1/19

CHRISTMAS GHOSTS AT THE PRIORY

Miss Eloise Granville is begrudgingly accepting of her arranged marriage to Viscount Garrick Forsythe — but when she discovers he is not aware of her infirmity, she is horrified. The wedding is only three weeks away, and it's far too late to cancel. Will he think he has been tricked? As Eloise anxiously awaits Garrick's arrival at St Cuthbert's Priory, the resident ghosts learn of the betrothal and unleash a fury that puts them both in grave danger. Will they find love amidst the chaos, or will circumstances push them apart?

FENELLA J. MILLER

CHRISTMAS GHOSTS AT THE PRIORY

Complete and Unabridged

LINFORD
Leicester

First published in Great Britain in 2018

First Linford Edition
published 2019

A catalogue record for this book is available
from the British Library.

ISBN 978–1–4448–4292–0

Published by
F. A. Thorpe (Publishing)
Anstey, Leicestershire

Set by Words & Graphics Ltd.
Anstey, Leicestershire
Printed and bound in Great Britain by
T. J. International Ltd., Padstow, Cornwall

This book is printed on acid-free paper

1

December, 1814.

'My lord, you are wanted in the study.' The butler bowed politely and stood aside to allow Garrick to precede him down the spacious corridor.

He had been expecting the summons and was bracing himself to accept the inevitable without protest. His grandfather, the Earl of Penston, had not long to live and was determined that his only surviving relative would be married before that day arrived.

Garrick was well aware he was delinquent in his duties to his name by not having stepped into parson's mousetrap before now. After all, a gentleman of his age was expected to be safely married to a suitable young lady by now, especially if one was the only heir to an earldom.

Indeed, he had tried to find himself a bride amongst the many fluttering, vacuous debutantes that had graced the London Season for the past few years but none of them would do. When he had reached his majority he had foolishly given his promise to his grandfather that he would marry the earl's choice without argument if he was still unwed at five and twenty.

Now he was hoist by his own petard and must fulfil his vow. God knows who had been selected for him — but he doubted whoever it was could be any less appealing than those he had rejected these past years.

The door to the study stood open and he strolled in without knocking knowing this would irritate the irascible old gentleman sitting behind the desk.

'Well, sir, I have made things simple for you. You will marry Miss Eloise Granville. She is the granddaughter of a dear friend of mine, Sir Thomas Granville, and has an ancient pedigree to match your own. She is yet to have a season which is fortunate for you, young man, as I have no doubt she would have been snapped up immediately.'

'Am I to know any more about my future wife, my lord?'

'She is seventeen years of age, an excellent horsewoman, and well-educated. She is pretty enough, and happy with the match. Her parents were killed in a carriage accident when she was small and she has grown up in the sole care of her grandparents.'

'Then we have one thing in common already. And when is our marriage to take place?'

'The first calling of the banns was yesterday and it will be a Christmas marriage. A double celebration for the family and yourself.'

'Devil take it! Am I not to meet the chit before I am obliged to bed her?' His grandparent ignored his indelicate remark.

'The announcement of your forthcoming nuptials will appear in The Times today. You will bring her here as soon as you are united.'

Garrick swallowed his anger with

difficulty. He was very fond of his only living relative; like the girl he was being forced to marry, he had been orphaned young and spent his entire life under the control of his grandfather.

'Then I had better return to my own estate and get my trunks packed. There are also other matters I must settle before I leave. Exactly where does Miss Granville reside?'

'No more than fifty miles from here and slightly less from your establishment. You will be married in their family chapel on the twenty-third of the month. You will remain there until Twelfth Night and then bring your bride here and reside with me until my demise.'

Penston Hall would be his, as would the title, so it made sense for him to make his home here. The girl he was obliged to marry was too young for the responsibility of running such a vast household — good God, she was scarcely out of the schoolroom.

'When am I expected at, what is it called? St Cuthbert's Priory? That is hardly an auspicious name.'

The old man chuckled. 'Ridiculous to live in a place so called. It is an ancient pile with many additions over the centuries and is like a rabbit warren. It is also said to be haunted by a variety of ghosts. Your stay will not be dull, I can assure you.'

'I shall take my leave, Grandfather, but will return if you need me.'

'Pish, my boy, I am not intending to kick the bucket for a few months more. If my legs still functioned I would accompany you as I would dearly love to see you married.'

'Then why can we not be married here? Presumably the banns have been read in our chapel as well?'

'They have, and if you had attended matins you would have heard them yourself. Why not send a letter by express to Sir Thomas and see if has any objection to having the ceremony here? He and Lady Granville are, as far as I'm aware, hale and hearty and would have no problems travelling.'

'If we rearrange it in this way then this house must be made more festive. Guests must be invited . . . '

'No, my boy, that will not do. I cannot abide a house party and dislike the old-fashioned way of decorating a house for Christmas. We shall leave things as they are. I shall ask the Rector to conduct a service of blessing on your union when you return with Eloise. That will be enough for me.'

'In which case, my lord, I shall consider that my true wedding day. Forgive me; I have business to attend to in town before I depart for St Cuthbert's Priory.'

He bowed to the old gentleman and he nodded in return. Garrick strode out and called for his horse to be fetched and his greatcoat, beaver and gloves to be brought. As he cantered down the drive he had much to mull over. What puzzled him most was why Sir Thomas should wish to marry his granddaughter off before she had had a season. Seventeen was too young, in his opinion, to enter into matrimony. It was a lifelong commitment, unbreakable but by death, so why would Eloise have agreed to marry a man she had never met and knew nothing about?

* * *

Eloise listened with growing incredulity to her grandparents. 'I am to marry this Viscount Forsyth without having set eyes on him and in three weeks' time?'

The grandparents exchanged glances. It was her grandmother who spoke soothingly to her. 'My dearest girl, you were adamant that you would not go to London for a season and find yourself a husband so we thought this would be easier for you.' Grandmama smiled. 'We are in our dotage, Eloise, and cannot hold parties and balls for you. However, Penston has been a friend of this family forever and he is in a similar position with his grandson. The opportunity seemed heaven sent.'

'I am only seventeen, why cannot I marry him when I reach my majority? I am not ready for the responsibilities and neither am I interested in producing infants for him. I take it that is why he is in such a rush to marry?'

Her grandfather hid his smile behind his hand at her remark but was forced to comment when he was fixed with a basilisk stare by his wife.

'I will be frank with you, my dear, the earl has heart failure and is unlikely to live for many more months. Lord Forsyth is the last surviving male in the family and it is imperative that he provides an heir as the estates are entailed.'

'Is he hideous? Is he a hardened gambler or a rake? Is that why he has failed to find himself a wife and must recourse to this nonsense?'

She knew her forthright speaking shocked them both but she was past caring if she offended them. She loved them dearly. They were octogenarians and could not be there to take care of her for many more years. They were doing what they thought was best for her and she could not fault them for their desire to see her settled.

'We would never have proposed you married anyone you could not like or that had a bad reputation. I have not seen him myself but have it on good authority that he stands more than two yards high, has an impressive width of shoulder and a handsome face.' Grandpapa looked to his wife for confirmation. She nodded.

'He has dark hair and blue eyes, an unusual combination. He has recently reached his twenty-fifth anniversary. He has no need of your fortune as they are a wealthy family.'

'The more I hear about him the less I understand why he should wish to marry a cripple like me when he could have the pick of the season.'

'Eloise, you must not speak of yourself in those terms. You have a limp which means you cannot dance, but in every other respect you are a beautiful young lady. I am sure he will take no notice of your slight imperfection.'

She stared at them in horror. 'He

does not know? He has been tricked into marrying someone like me. How could you do that?'

She pushed herself to her feet and wished she could run out but was forced to make her usual slow, uneven passage to the door. The banns were being called today, the announcement had been sent to the newspaper, it was too late to warn him he had been sold a pig in a poke.

Only when riding her gelding, Emperor, did she feel the equal of anyone else. When she was younger and recovering from the horrendous injury, whilst also trying to come to terms with the loss of her parents, she had often wished she had also died.

Her leg still gave her pain but she suffered more from the loss of mobility, and the fact that she had to endure the pitying glances of those who saw her hobbling about the place. When she was stationary no one would know, she was a tall girl, slender but with the necessary feminine curves front and back. The good Lord had seen fit to bless her with an abundance of nut-brown hair and even she did not need convincing that her emerald eyes were her finest feature.

Her apartment was on the ground floor and in one of the oldest parts of the Priory — no one bothered her there as the corridors and chambers were haunted by past residents. She was at home with her spectral companions and they were her solace and her company. She had no friends on the earthly plane.

Her servants were those that had served her since before her parents died. Tom and his wife Polly took care of her well and kept her rooms and belongings immaculate. They had never been blessed with children of their own and she was their substitute daughter. The ghosts held no fears for them either.

The door to this ancient part of the building was kept closed — her grand-mother insisted it was because of the draught but everyone knew it was to keep the ghosts contained. The door swung open as she approached.

'Thank you, Brother Francis, I am most obliged to you for your courtesy.'

'And I to you, it is a pleasure to be of some small service.' The ghostly shape shimmered and dissolved until she could no longer see him, but she was aware he remained, as always, guarding the door.

She was met by the comforting presence of her maid. 'Miss Eloise, what has upset you? You tell your old Polly all about it. You sit here, my love, and I'll fetch you some coffee and a nice slice of the plum cake you're so fond of.'

'Just coffee, thank you, Polly. I'm going to change into my habit afterwards so could you please ask Tom to saddle the horses for us?'

'You go into the parlour, Miss Eloise, there's a fine fire burning in there. The company is restless today, I reckon they know something untoward is about to happen.' This was how she referred to their ghostly companions. Polly bustled away unperturbed by having to literally walk through three other spectres.

'Come with me, brothers, and I will explain why the atmosphere here has changed, and not for the better.'

If anyone had come in whilst she was speaking they would have thought her fit for a lunatic asylum as her companions were only visible to her. Polly and Tom sensed they were there and sometimes said they caught a glimpse of something from the corner of their eyes, but she was the fortunate one they revealed themselves to.

These three apparitions were monks who had once resided here. They had been cruelly murdered when the monasteries had been dissolved by King Henry and the magnificent building taken over by one of his favoured courtiers. Fortunately, they were not in any way destructive or unpleasant — at least not to her.

They floated around her listening to her woes. By the end of her tale they had turned an ominous shade of grey. She knew from past experience that when they became dark in colour the more destructive they could be. They were perfectly capable of invading the rest of the house but chose to remain in the ancient corridors and rooms they had inhabited when they had been mortal.

'You cannot marry this man, we do not allow it. You belong here with us where we can protect you from harm.' The speaker was the most vocal of the trio, Brother James, and he was also the most capable of doing harm. Sometimes he became so solid he was almost real. He could move objects violently and cause upset to anyone in his vicinity when he was angry.

'I have no choice; my grandparents have already set things in motion. I doubt that he's any more thrilled than I am by this arranged marriage . . . '

'He cannot marry you if he is dead. When he sets foot in the Priory we will take care of the matter for you. Then you can remain here and be our conduit to the human world.'

For the first time since she had encountered these ghosts Eloise was afraid to be in their company. It took her a moment to regain her composure. 'That will not be necessary, but I thank you for your concern, Brother. I have no wish for him or anyone else to be harmed in any way by you and your companions.'

The three shapes merged into one. The hair on the back of her neck stood up. They had never done this before and up until this moment she had never felt herself to be in any danger. Then the door swung open and Polly came in carrying a tray.

'My word, miss, it's cold in here today. Sit by the fire, move away from the door and drink your coffee.'

Before she could warn her, the tray flew from Polly's hands and smashed to the stone floor.

'Get out of here. You're not welcome. I don't wish to communicate with you again today.' For some strange reason if she told them directly to vanish they had no option but to do so. Why she should have this connection with the other world she had no idea, but until today she had been grateful and thought herself blessed.

She was about to drop to her knees and help her maid collect the broken shards of crockery but was waved away. 'No, clearing up is my job. Something's upset the company today. I hope you sent them packing.'

'I have, Polly. I just told them I'm to be married in three weeks and will then have to live elsewhere. I realise now that was an error. It would have been better to pretend everything was going to remain the same.' She shuddered as she considered what mayhem the four monks could wreak if they decided to venture back into the central section of the Priory. This was occupied by her grandparents and would be where Lord Forsyth would be staying too.

* * *

Garrick made the necessary arrange-ments for his departure in two days' time and then set out for London and the unpleasant task of severing the connection with his mistress. Lady Sarah Dunstable, a wealthy young widow, had been his *chere aimee* for the past three years and he knew her to be a jealous woman. He was certain if he had not been in a passionate and tempestuous relationship with her he might well have been more accommodating when it came to selecting a bride.

Sarah was a few years his senior, had been married briefly to an ancient peer who had left her a wealthy woman. He was not her first lover, and he was certain would not be her last. She enjoyed the company of gentlemen and had no intention of giving up her reckless independence by marrying for a second time.

He had a friend who had married under similar circumstances himself but he had not ended the relationship and continued to visit his mistress leaving his unfortunate young wife at home with the infants.

However much he might dislike the

idea of marrying this girl he would not be unfaithful to her once the knot was tied. He would do his best to be a good husband and was certain that in time he could persuade her to fall in love with him. This would make life easier for his bride and no doubt for himself. Life was simpler for a gentleman in these circumstances as he could remove himself from the situation if he found it unpleasant and this option was not open to his wife.

He travelled in a closed carriage as he always did when he visited Sarah — he had no wish to advertise his presence at her home. As always, the coachman turned the horses expertly through the archway and halted in the turning circle. A waiting groom kicked down the steps and opened the door.

Garrick ignored the various members of staff who bowed and opened doors for him. He was not there to fraternise with servants, but to speak to Sarah and it was not something he was looking forward to.

She greeted him with her usual blinding smile. She was a voluptuous beauty, he was going to miss what he had shared with her over these past few years.

'My darling boy, what brings you here when you are not expected until next week?'

Then she noticed he had not handed over his outdoor garments, was still holding his gloves in one hand and had his beaver under his arm. Her expression changed in an instant. Her eyes narrowed and she viewed him with disfavour.

'I see. I am to be given my *conge*. I suppose I must be grateful you have come to break the connection in person and have not done so by a letter.'

'I am to be married in three weeks' time, my lady, and have no option but to say farewell. I have loved every minute I have spent with you but we both knew one day it would come to this. I am just sorry I could not give you more warning.'

Her smile returned. 'Good heavens, my love, there's no need to look so glum. Marry as you must, then return to me when you can. I'm prepared to wait.'

'No, I intend to remain faithful to my wife. I am sorry, I know that might seem unnecessary, but I believe the vows I'm going to take must be held to.' He dipped into his inside pocket and placed his parting gift on the mantelshelf. He did not dare to risk approaching her. She was of a mercurial temperament and likely to try and hit him with the nearest heavy object.

'I hope this will be some compensation for my absence.' He bowed and hastily backed out before she could react. Hopefully when she looked inside the leather box she would be mollified by the splendid diamond bracelet that he had purchased for her. He had never given her family jewels, had always had them made especially for her.

His carriage had now turned, the horses were stamping and tossing their heads eager to be on their way. Now he had severed his link with her he was ready to drive down to meet his future wife with a clear conscience. He had no intention of laying with her until after the marriage was blessed in front of his grandfather. This would give him approximately five weeks to woo her — with luck that would be sufficient.

2

Eloise did not remain inside for a second tray of coffee to be fetched to her. She needed to get out, have a wild gallop on Emperor and forget who she was. Being in constant pain from the leg that had been so badly broken meant she was never able to forget she was an orphan and crippled. The fact that she could communicate with the spirit world was usually something she revelled in. From today she was beginning to think it might be a curse rather than a blessing.

Tom always accompanied her when she rode in case she needed a gate opening or took a tumble and was unable to remount. His hunter could keep pace with her horse and he enjoyed the excursions as much as she did. He remained a fit and healthy man despite his increasing years.

'Where to today, Miss Eloise?'

'Anywhere as long as I can gallop and take a jump or two.' She rode astride as hooking her damaged leg around the pommel of a side-saddle was impossible. They never ventured off the estate so the neighbours could not possibly be offended by her outrageous behaviour.

There was no time to dwell on her worries — as always, thundering about the countryside on her gelding took her full concentration and allowed her to feel whole again. Eventually they drew rein to let the horses walk and cool down before they returned to their stables.

'That was exactly what I needed. I expect Polly has told you I'm to be married to a Viscount Forsyth.'

'It's all a bit sudden like, miss, but Sir Thomas wants only the best for you. As long as Polly and I can come with you, it makes no nevermind to us where we are.'

'That's the problem, Tom, I have no idea what sort of gentleman he might be, or if he will allow me to bring my own staff to wherever I am going to be living. I don't think my grandparents have actually met him, therefore, they are relying entirely on the word of his grandfather that he is a suitable match for me. I would not be so upset if they had told him the truth. He cannot back out any more than I can and I know that he will not wish to marry me once he sees . . . '

'Now that's enough of that, young lady, you're beautiful inside and out and I defy any gentleman of sense not to realise that the moment he sets eyes on you.'

'The ghosts are upset and threatening to murder him in order to keep me with them. I am at a loss to know what to do about that. If I tell my future husband I can communicate with spirits he will be even more appalled that he has to marry me.'

Suddenly Emperor shied at a pheasant that flew up under his hooves. He cannoned into Tom's mount and her companion vanished into the hedgerow. By the time she had calmed her own horse his hunter had bolted down the path.

'Are you injured, Tom?' She thought it unlikely as she could hear him cursing and swearing in the middle of the hawthorn hedge.

'I ain't hurt, miss, but I reckon I'm stuck fast in these blooming bushes. The more I struggle the worse it gets.'

'We need a couple of strong men to pull the branches beside. Fortunately, we're only half a mile from home. I'll fetch help.'

The bushes moved and he managed to part them sufficiently for her to see his face. She was shocked to see so much blood trickling down his cheeks. What had seemed like a minor incident was nothing of the sort.

'Please, Tom, remain still or you will receive further lacerations. Here, take my handkerchief and hold it against your forehead. You have a nasty gash which is bleeding copiously.' She edged

Emperor closer so she could lean down and pass the object to him.

'Don't you be worrying about me; a few scratches won't hurt your old Tom.'

'I'll be as quick as I can. I hope to catch your horse as well and will return with him.'

The gelding responded to her touch and sprung into an extended canter, she pushed him into a gallop and covered the distance in minutes. There was a carriage trundling up the drive and she thundered past it, too worried to give the occupant any heed.

She yelled the name of the head groom as she pulled her mount to a rearing halt. The man appeared instantly, his face etched with concern.

'Tom is stuck in a hedge and has several nasty cuts. He cannot extricate himself without assistance. Has his horse come home yet?'

'No, miss, no sign of him. I'll come with Jethro, together we can get him out easy enough. I'll send one of the boys to look for his horse. Tom can ride with me for such a short journey.'

She walked her horse around the turning circle whilst she waited for Ned and Jethro to appear. There were more than half a dozen riding horses kept in the stables as well as two teams to pull the various carriages.

In less than ten minutes the two men joined her. She led the way at a canter, again flying past the carriage that had by now almost reached the final stretch of the drive. This time she was aware there was a gentleman sitting inside. He raised his hand in salute and smiled.

The only visitor they were expecting was the viscount. He was indeed a handsome man and her heart lifted at the thought that he had seen her at her best.

★   ★   ★

When the carriage had slowed to pass through the gates Garrick had looked around with interest. There was no sign of the Priory, only endless parkland scattered with ancient trees and with several herds of red deer attempting to graze on the sparse winter grass.

The long drive curved round and then he could see the full glory of the edifice. He was impressed. There was a magnificent archway which must have been the original entrance to the Priory and adjacent to this was a row of equally ancient buildings, all built from similar golden sandstone. A single-storey meandered across the courtyard until it met the main structure.

Instinctively he grabbed onto the strap at the sound of a galloping horse approaching from the rear. A massive black gelding raced past and he caught a glimpse of the rider. This must be his future wife and the earl had not been wrong when he had said she was a good horsewoman.

Did she always travel at that speed or was there something untoward taking place? He settled back on the squabs, intrigued by his first few glimpses of Eloise. There was no time for niceties, he would address her by her given name and ask her to do the same for him. They had only three weeks to establish some sort of rapport before they would be obliged to commit themselves to a lifetime together.

It was a comfort to know they had one other thing in common — the love of fast horses. The team pulling his carriage were fatigued after the long journey despite having had overnight to recover. He had told his coachman to complete the journey at a walk so his horses would be cool enough to be fed and watered immediately.

He sincerely hoped there was a horse here up to his weight. Despite the fact that it was December the weather was surprisingly clement and so far there had been no snow and the ground remained firm but unfrozen.

When they were within a hundred yards of his destination he saw Eloise and two grooms galloping back the way she had just come. This time he leaned forward waved and smiled and she saw him and laughed. She was an original

— was it possible that he had found the perfect match for him?

The huge oriel window was the best he'd ever seen. Penston Hall was considered an impressive building, the height of modernity, having been constructed by his great-grandfather on the ruins of the old house. This had been razed to the ground by a fire. However, he was forced to admit that St Cuthbert's Priory was the most magnificent edifice he had ever set eyes on.

As expected the butler and housekeeper were there to greet him. He had no doubt offended their sensibilities by not sending his luggage ahead with his valet. Foster had travelled on the box and willingly acted as under-coachman. His man didn't enjoy being cooped up inside a carriage and was an indifferent horseman.

'My lord, the master has asked if you would join him in his study as soon as you have refreshed yourself.'

'I'll see him immediately. Direct me to him.'

Everywhere he looked there was evidence of this building's provenance. There were exquisite tapestries hanging on the walls, suits of armour, a whole array of ancient weapons. This entrance hall deserved more of his attention but it could wait until he had spoken to his host.

The liveried footman bowed and led him down a wide, flagstone corridor with mullioned windows on one side, that overlooked a splendid inner court-yard, and stopped outside an arched doorway.

'There is no need to announce me.' Garrick strode past the servant. He paused and bowed to the elderly gentleman sitting in an armchair in front of the fire.

'Forgive me, my lord, if I do not rise. I am not at all well today.'

He moved swiftly and took the chair opposite. 'Sir Thomas, my grandfather was unaware that you are infirm. I hope this is a temporary situation.'

'Sadly, my boy, it is not. You will not tell my granddaughter, she has no idea that my days are numbered as are those of your grandfather. My dear wife, fortunately, is in better case and I need to be assured that you will take care of her after my demise.'

This was not how Garrick had thought his first meeting with his future relative would go. 'You have my word, sir. Although I will not lie for you if your granddaughter asks me directly about your health. I can see now why there is this urgency for Eloise and me to be married.

'I saw my future wife in the park. I believe there might have been an accident of some sort from the urgency with which she and the two grooms departed.'

'If it was anything serious I would have been informed. I must tell you that Eloise is not overjoyed at this arrangement. She is resigned but not happy.'

'How could she be? To be obliged to marry a gentleman she has never met is enough to upset any young lady of sensibility.'

Sir Thomas chuckled. 'My grand-daughter's reservations are because she has no wish to leave here, I think marrying you — or any other suitable gentleman — is not her main concern. I must ask you if you will agree to remain here until I have departed from this world.'

'My grandfather has a congestion of the heart. His physician is sanguine that he will survive for several months. Nevertheless, I have given him my word I shall return with Eloise by the middle of January so our marriage can be blessed in our family chapel.'

'I have a canker in my chest. My doctor has said that I shall be lucky to survive for more than a few weeks after the new year. Once I am safely buried you can leave with my dearest Emma and Eloise and return to Penston with my blessing.

'I wish this to be a memorable Christmas for my girls. I intend to have the house decorated with as many frills and furbelows, baubles and ribbons, greenery and candles as my staff can lay their hands on. Do not look so despondent, my boy, I am in my eighty-fifth year and ready to meet my Maker.'

There was further conversation about what had been planned to celebrate the wedding, and the twelve days of Christmas. It was a horrible coincidence that both Eloise and he were going to lose their grandfathers in the new year. This was one connection he sincerely wished they did not share.

'I shall leave you now, sir, and change out of my disarray. I apologise for appearing as I am but I was eager to make your acquaintance and have the matter settled.'

'What did you think of my Eloise, my lord? She is a lovely young lady, is she not?'

'Indeed, she is. Have no fear, I'll make this work for both of us. I could wish she was a few years older, but I can assure you I'll not ask her to do anything she does not want until she is ready.'

This was his oblique way of telling Sir Thomas he would not demand his conjugal rights the moment the knot was tied.

'Thank you. I know I am leaving my dearest granddaughter in safe hands. My wife will be waiting to greet you in the green drawing room. We rarely use the formal chamber as it is too big for just three of us. I shall see you at dinner. We keep country hours here and dine at five o'clock.'

Garrick bowed and left the study with more to think about than he had expected. Something puzzled him and it was the fact that Sir Thomas had not thought it relevant to inform the earl that he too was not long for this world.

He was going to find it difficult to keep this information from Eloise. Surely, she had noticed the yellow tinge to her grandfather's face and his extreme thinness?

His palatial apartment was everything it should be, if a tad old-fashioned for his taste. He had an enormous tester bed, the curtains of which were heavy brocade — these would be necessary, as an icy wind blew through the room as he stood there admiring it.

The hair on the back of his neck stood up for some reason. He shrugged this off and left Foster to set out his clean garments whilst he inspected the sitting room. The cold draught mysteriously followed him and he shivered. The enormous fireplace had a cheery fire burning brightly, so why did he feel cold?

He pushed these fancies to one side, stripped off his soiled shirt and replaced it with a clean one. He preferred to tie his own neckcloth and shave himself.

'Allow me to assist you to put on your topcoat, my lord. I have selected the dark blue as it complements your waistcoat.'

He shrugged it on and waited impatiently for his valet to smooth it across his shoulders. His boots were now pristine and he was ready to descend and meet the lady of the house. He was even more eager to make the acquaintance of the woman he was going to spend the rest of his life with. He was intrigued to know what had transpired to make her rush about the countryside with such abandon. It had not escaped his notice that she was riding astride — that was something that would cease once she was his concern.

* * *

With the assistance of the two grooms Tom was able to free himself without further harm. He scrambled up behind Ned, and Eloise led the three of them back at a more decorous pace than she had arrived.

'You must ask Bates to put a couple of sutures into your wound, Tom. It might well go putrid if it isn't stitched.'

'I could do that, miss, but I reckon my Polly can do as good a job as the housekeeper. It won't be the first time she's patched me up.'

She smiled at him. 'As long as it's

done. I could not manage without you. Viscount Forsyth has arrived in my absence. He waved and smiled as I galloped past so I'm inclined to think he might be a reasonable gentleman.'

This conversation was carried on as if the two grooms were both invisible and deaf. It might be better not to discuss such matters in front of them.

She completed the remainder of the journey in silence. She guided her horse to the block so she could dismount without overbalancing. A stableboy was waiting to take the animal's reins and lead him away. She entered her own domain through the side door with Tom close behind her. She must quickly wash and change into something more suitable for her first meeting with her future husband.

Polly had everything waiting for her. 'I've put out the burgundy velvet, the one with a high neck and long sleeves. The weather's turned right cold today and you'll need something warm.'

'Thank you, I can manage this very

well on my own. Tom needs your ministrations more than I do at the moment.'

Within half an hour she was free from the taint of the stable, freshly dressed in her favourite winter gown and on her way to the main part of the house. There was something not quite right and she could not put her finger on it. Then she realised the doorkeeper was no longer at his position.

Why had he abandoned his post? A shiver of apprehension ran through her as she recalled the words spoken by the ghosts. At times like these she hated the fact that she could not run — for some reason she believed his lordship was in deadly danger and only she could keep him safe.

3

Garrick finished his inspection of the apartment he would be using for the next few weeks and turned to his valet who was hovering in the bedchamber doorway.

'What is it?'

'There's something downright strange about this place. I've been closing doors and minutes later they are open again. I reckon the Priory is haunted.'

He had been about to dismiss Foster's claim as nonsense when it felt as if an icy hand had brushed across his face. Like most sensible fellows he had no time for superstition, was not even sure that he believed there was a Supreme Being controlling their every move, but there was something about the Priory that was making him reconsider.

'Are you telling me you wish to leave here? I cannot do so, obviously, but I will accept your resignation if that is what suits you.'

His man gaped at him. 'No, my lord, I'm happy in my position. I just wanted to warn you to expect the unexpected whilst we're here. I'm not afraid of the odd ghost or two — only to be expected seeing as this is such an ancient building.'

'I'm forced to agree with you, although it goes against everything I believed in before I came here. We must just hope these spirits are not malevolent.'

'Malevolent or not, my lord, they cannot hurt the living. Maybe I need to fetch us both some garlic from the kitchen to be sure.'

'Not for me, Foster, I cannot abide the smell. I shall recite the Lord's Prayer — that should keep them away.'

This was a ridiculous conversation to be having and he was smiling as he left his sitting room. He would ask Eloise to give him the full tour of this extraordinary place but first he must make his bow to Lady Granville.

He paused every now and again to look at family portraits, and admire ancient artefacts, as he traversed the long passageway. The light filtered through the multi coloured glass of the huge oriel window making the gallery that led to the stairs a magical place.

The ceiling of the great hall was painted blue and everywhere he looked there were gold stars twinkling down at him. Here the ceiling was double height at least and he stood at the head of the staircase looking upwards.

He was startled by the sudden shout from below. 'Take care, my lord, there's danger behind you.'

He had no time to reply as at that precise moment a massive battleaxe flew from the wall. He threw himself backwards and the lethal object landed blade first inches from his feet.

Without that warning he would have been dead.

He had never seen anything like it. The axe hadn't fallen from the hooks, something had removed it and thrown it at his head. His heart was pounding. Cold sweat trickled between his shoulder blades.

Then he heard halting footsteps and Eloise arrived in the gallery. She was ashen, as shocked as he at his near demise. He scrambled to his feet.

Only then did he notice she was lame. It bothered him not one jot, but he was puzzled this information had not been given to him.

He walked quickly towards her so she did not have to move herself. He held out his hands and without hesitation she took them. They were not white and silky-smooth, but tanned, slightly rough and remarkably strong for a young lady.

'If you had not called out, Eloise, I would be singing with the angels now. I take it the resident spectres are not delighted to have me here.'

Her eyes widened and her fingers tightened around his. 'They are not, my lord . . . '

'No, my name is Garrick. We are to

be married soon and I wish us to be friends before that happens.'

Her smile made her lovely face even more beautiful — she had the most spectacular green eyes. He counted himself a fortunate man to be marrying her.

'Garrick, they don't want me to leave here and intend to murder you in order to stop our nuptials. They are the ghosts of the murdered monks who lived here hundreds of years ago. Unfortunately, I am able to communicate with them and they consider me their property.'

'I have already encountered them in my apartment. I am supposed to be meeting your grandmother, but we need to talk first. Let us return to my sitting room. There can be no objection to you being there alone with me as we're already betrothed.'

He pulled her hand through his arm and she made no objection. Her gait was more even when she could lean on him for support.

'How did you come to be injured, my dear?'

She told him briefly about the accident that had taken her parents from her and almost her own life. 'The physician did not set the bones correctly and that is why I limp so badly and have constant pain.' She looked at him and there were tears in her eyes. 'I should not have said that — I am making more fuss than is necessary.'

'I broke my leg when I was a stripling and our personal physician did an excellent job of setting it. If you're prepared to undergo an hour or two of excruciating pain I believe he might be able to straighten your leg . . .'

'Are you telling me you think I would no longer be a cripple?'

'You are no more a cripple than I am, Eloise. You will not refer to yourself in such derogatory terms again.' He frowned but she saw through him. Her eyes sparkled and something inside him changed.

'I see how it is to be, sir, you wish me to be a subservient wife and follow your every command to the letter.'

With his free hand he raised hers to his lips and kissed her knuckles. He was delighted to see her cheeks flush at his action. 'Indeed I do, sweetheart. I can see we're going to deal famously together now you understand the situation.'

Her laughter made his pulse unexpectedly skip a beat. His sitting room was empty and he led her to the *chaise longue* that stood in front of the roaring fire. 'We shall sit here together and further our acquaintance.'

★　★　★

Eloise was never flustered but something about this charming gentleman made her feel most unsettled. He had almost been beheaded by one of the monks and had taken it in his stride. Her limp appeared to be a mere bagatelle to him and the sick dread she had carried inside since she had been told about her forthcoming marriage began to dissipate.

'To return to the subject of my leg. I gather from what you said that the surgeon will be obliged to break my leg in order to reset it — do I have that right?'

'I need to say something to you first before you even consider the suggestion. I don't want you to do this for me because I am not in any way perturbed by your lack of mobility. You must only do it for yourself. If you think the acute pain would be worth it, then I shall set things in motion. I would certainly think twice about undergoing such a procedure myself so will think none the worse of you if you decline.'

His kindness endeared him to her. 'I would endure any amount of agony in order to be whole again, to be able to run, to negotiate staircases without pain . . . '

He said something most impolite and she could not hold back her giggle. He raised an eyebrow and she laughed out loud. 'You must not use such language in front of my grandmama. She will have a fit of the vapours.'

'I beg your pardon, unforgivable behaviour on my part. I shall endeavour to keep my expletives to myself in future. I was upset that you had been forced to come upstairs on my behalf.'

'Fiddlesticks to that! I do what I must and try not to let my infirmity rule my life. Now, we must talk about the monks.'

'I had no notion members of the spirit world could move objects in that way. Every wall is festooned with weapons and dangerous items, I believe I had better borrow the shield that hangs beneath the window and walk about with it above my head in future.'

'How can you make light of it? Until today I thought these ghosts my friends. I sympathised with them being trapped halfway between this world and the next by some quirk of fate. Now I know them to be dangerous and far from benign.'

He stretched out his long, booted legs to the flames and smiled at her. 'I take it that the entire household is aware the Priory is haunted?'

'Of course they are, but no one talks about it, especially my grandparents. When I moved into the downstairs chambers, the ones that in their original form were once occupied by these monks, they ceased to wander about the place causing upset and hysteria to the staff. No one else is able to communicate with them in the way that I do.'

'Can't you tell them to remain in your chambers?'

'I can send them away from my presence and they have no alternative but to go. I'd no idea they would then decide to reoccupy this part of the Priory.' She reached into a hidden pocket in the side of her skirt and withdrew a large gold crucifix. 'Here, you must wear this at all times of the day and night. I believe it will protect you.'

He held out his hand and she dropped the cross and chain into it. 'My valet, Foster, suggested I have garlic in my pocket. I much prefer your alternative.'

'Allow me to fasten it around your

neck. If you put it in your pocket you might well forget to wear it at night.' She leaned forward. 'All the staff have one about their person somewhere.'

He sat up; her eyes followed the passage of his legs as he moved them. The anatomy of a gentleman had never interested her before but for some inexplicable reason she could not keep back her laugh and he looked at her with interest.

'What are you finding so amusing?'

Scalding colour flooded her cheeks and she couldn't look at him. She swallowed her embarrassment and raised her head. 'I have never spent time alone with any gentleman, let alone someone as personable as you.'

'And you find this funny?' His query was soft, a strange expression in his eyes.

She wished the floor would open up and swallow her and that she had never started this conversation. No — she would not be coy about this. In less than three weeks she would be his wife.

She swallowed the lump in her

throat. 'What I found funny is the fact that I was admiring the length of your legs and could not think why I should be interested — then I remembered that . . . that . . . ' She was incapable of finishing her sentence.

'That when we're married everything will change between us. There's something you need to know, sweetheart, we shall have a second marriage service once we join the earl at Penston Hall. I shall consider that the start of our life together.'

For a moment she didn't take his meaning then a wave of relief flooded through her. She had no clear idea what took place in the marriage bed as her grandmother had made no attempt to explain. What Polly had told her sounded so extraordinary she'd dismissed it. The longer she had to come to terms with what she must do with him the happier she would be.

'When do you intend that we depart for your home?'

'At the end of January, no sooner than

that. As you are aware my grandfather will not survive for many more months so we must be back before he becomes too unwell.'

Her eyes filled. 'I should like to stay until my own grandfather dies. I fear that might well be quite soon. Grandmama and I pretend we're not aware of his failing health, we do not discuss it even between ourselves, but one only has to look at him to know he cannot live for many more weeks.'

Her misery at the thought she would lose her much loved grandparent welled up. She was trying to push back the sobs, to maintain an outward calm, when he scooped her up and pulled her onto his lap.

'Cry as much as you want to, little one, I'm here to take care of you and your grandmother now.'

★   ★   ★

As Eloise shivered and sobbed in his arms, Garrick rubbed her back and murmured words of encouragement and comfort. He thanked the Almighty that he hadn't found himself a bride as then he would never have met this extraordinary girl.

She was strong, courageous, intelligent and could talk to ghosts. The way she had mentioned this, as if it was of no more import than being able to play a hand of Whist, astonished him. If she hadn't been lame she would have been presented last year and already betrothed to someone else. That didn't bear thinking of.

They might only have met each other an hour ago but already he thought of her as his to protect. He passed her his handkerchief and eventually she blew her nose noisily, mopped her eyes and relaxed in his embrace.

'I was dreading meeting you, Garrick, but you've surprised me. Instead of being an unmitigated disaster for both of us I believe our grandparents have done us a favour.' She twisted and smiled trustingly up at him. 'I believe I must remove myself from your lap. I cannot fathom how I came to be here in the first place.'

Reluctantly he lifted her and placed her a safe distance from him. She was a stunningly beautiful girl and he was going to find it difficult keeping to his promise to remain from her bed for the first weeks of their marriage.

'You needed comfort and it's my role to provide it. The next few weeks are going to be difficult for both of us as we're going to lose someone we hold dear. If we support each other in our grief we will survive and recover quicker.'

'You're right and I thank you for allowing me to cry all over your fresh shirt. Grandpapa is determined to have the house decorated. He insists it's to celebrate our wedding but I think he wants something to occupy his final weeks and distract us from his deteriorating health.'

'I've never seen things done in the old-fashioned way and am looking forward to gathering greenery and so on. You must involve your grandmother too, things must be so much harder for her.'

They were carefully avoiding the far more difficult conversation that they must have. Talking about ghosts was not something he had expected to be doing.

After a further ten minutes of inconsequential chit-chat she sighed. 'I know, we must come to some decision with regards to the brothers.'

'Brothers? Oh, I take it you're referring to the ghostly monks.'

'I am, of course, and despite the fact they have no corporeal body they've already demonstrated they can cause real harm.'

'Presumably you have a family priest — can he not exorcise them?'

'The subject has never been discussed. After I took residence in their wing they no longer haunted the main part of the Priory. That was three years ago. When I achieved my fourteenth year I was deemed old enough to set up my own household somewhere that didn't require me to hobble up several flights of stairs.'

'Then when you leave will the ghosts

no longer be able to haunt this place? Do you know what arrangements your grandfather has made for the estate?'

'Everything is left to me — which means on my marriage to you it will be your responsibility. If we have more than one son there will be something for all of them to inherit. I don't know if you were told but I also have a substantial annuity that remains in my control.'

She waited expectantly for his reaction to this extraordinary announcement.

'I'm glad that you'll be financially independent. I cannot imagine you would enjoy asking me for permission every time you wished to purchase something for yourself.'

Her delightful laughter warmed him as it had before. 'You don't fully understand what I've told you. I'm independently wealthy — my income is in the region of five thousand pounds a year. I'm not talking about pin money.'

'God's teeth! Indeed, you are not. Why did Sir Thomas think you needed a private income?'

'Kindly moderate your language, my lord, I do not enjoy hearing such things.' Her words were strict but her eyes danced.

He nodded. 'For a second time I beg your pardon for my intemperate outburst. But you are yet to answer my question, madam.'

'The money is not from him but from my mother. She inherited this fund from her mother and it is passed from daughter to daughter. I shall leave it to any daughter that I have.'

This was the second reference she'd made to children. The thought of what must take place before any arrived made him bitterly regret his vow to not consummate the marriage until after the second ceremony had taken place in front of his grandfather.

'And if we have more than one daughter?'

'Then, my lord, it will be divided between them. This also is a family tradition.'

Once more the conversation had wandered from the subject that must be addressed. It would be better to discuss the ghosts and take his mind off bedroom sport.

'Eloise, I have yet to make the acquaintance of your grandmother and she must be appalled by my lack of manners. That said, we need to come to some decision about how I'm to avoid being impaled by an ancient sword or struck on the head by a claymore.'

'I can think of only one solution, Garrick. They'll not harm me, so you must remain constantly at my side whilst you're here. I'll move into the adjoining bedchamber today — I care not what rules of etiquette we break — that way I can be sure they won't hurt you.'

'You'll only do this if you agree that I can carry you up and down the stairs. No, my love, do not frown at me. I know, because you told me so, how much pain it gives you to climb them.' He waited until she nodded before continuing. 'I cannot see your grandparents agreeing to such a breach of protocol. How will you explain your wish to move into my apartment three weeks before our nuptials?'

'Fiddlesticks to that! They will both be so delighted we've taken to each other that they'll not object.'

He rose smoothly to his feet and lifted her to hers. 'I'll agree not to use improper language if you desist from your ridiculous fiddlesticks expression.'

She tilted her head to one side and placed a fingertip on her lips in a parody of a silly debutante. 'La, my lord, I shall have to give that weighty matter due consideration. If I cannot fiddlesticks then what should I do instead?'

4

'You are an original — Miss Granville
— and I can see I'm going to be run
ragged by you. I assume the connecting
bedchamber is already prepared for
your use?'

'Your assumptions are correct, my lord,
and I can see I'm going to be married to
a gentleman with sharp wits and a ready
understanding.'

Laughing together they headed for
the gallery. A brush of cold wind ruffled
her hair and immediately she moved
closer to him and he put his arm
around her waist.

'I felt that too. Can you see them?
Are they speaking to you?'

'Now that you mention it, I can
neither see nor hear them. I believe they
can only materialise when in the old
part of the building where I live.'

His rich, deep chuckle was an

attractive sound. 'Isn't this part of the Priory hundreds of years old?'

'It is, but recent compared to the part that the monks used to dwell in.' Having his support meant she could almost walk without limping and certainly without pain.

As they reached the gallery he put his other arm underneath her knees and continued to stride forward as if carrying nothing heavier than a bag of feathers. She might be slender but certainly was no lightweight.

'I'm beginning to think that having a husband of your size is an excellent choice. I'll expect you to carry me about the place whenever I require it, sir, as it obviously causes you no difficulty. Imagine if you'd been a short, stout gentleman. What a disaster that would have been for me!'

He lowered his head and whispered in her ear. 'I enjoy carrying you, sweetheart, and cannot wait until I can transport you to my bed.'

Her blush travelled from her toes to

her crown and she could think of nothing sensible to say in reply. How could they be so close after so short a space of time? Three days ago, she'd never heard of him and now she was halfway to finding him a most desirable partner.

Several times on their descent she was aware they were being accompanied by the ghosts but nothing untoward took place and they arrived safely in the great hall.

'Look at that, the battleaxe has already been replaced.'

'I think the damage to the floor-boards in the gallery might take longer to remove.'

'Please put me down now, I can walk almost normally if you keep your arm around my waist so I can lean my weight on you.'

He did as she asked. She'd never been in such close proximity to anyone before, let alone to a gentleman who was almost a stranger.

She directed him to the smaller

drawing room that was used when the family were alone. There would be two dozen or more guests arriving to celebrate her wedding in the next week or two and the formal room would come into action then.

A footman had hurried ahead and opened the door. 'Grandmama, I've brought my future husband to meet you. I must apologise for his tardy arrival. I shall explain everything to you.'

Her grandmother was no more than a year or two younger than her husband but wore her years well. She was tiny but her robust character made one think she was a person of greater stature.

'Welcome, my lord, to St Cuthbert's Priory. I cannot tell you how happy it makes me that you and Eloise are already so close.'

He released his hold but remained beside her so his bulk was supporting her. He bowed. 'I'm delighted to be here, my lady, and I thank you for your kind welcome.'

Formalities over, Eloise gestured with

her head that they take the sofa opposite her grandmother. Once they were comfortable she decided to no longer prevaricate about the situation.

When she had completed her explanation her ancient relative looked decidedly shocked. 'I'd no idea that the spectres could be violent. Of course, your grandfather and I are well aware you're not alone in your chambers but as long as you were happy with your ghostly companions then we thought it safe for you to remain.'

'So you see, Grandmama, why I have no option but to move into Garrick's apartment. If I don't do so then they might succeed in their efforts to murder him before our wedding.'

'Your grandfather will not approve but I agree with you. Heaven knows what our house guests will think of the situation.'

He spoke for the first time on this subject. 'As long as you and Sir Thomas are content then no one else's opinion matters, my lady. Do the guests sleep on the same side of the Priory as family?'

'No, my lord, they reside in the other wing. You, of course, are on the family side.'

'Exactly so. Therefore, I can see no difficulty as they'll not be aware of our outrageous sleeping arrangements.'

'It is most inconvenient having ghosts floating about the place in this way, Eloise. Can you not control your friends? Demand they remain in their own premises?'

'I think they have their own plans, Grandmama. They're well aware that once I'm gone they'll be trapped and unable to communicate with anyone.'

'I think it's time we spoke of the other matter, my dear girl. Your grandfather is not long for this world, and when he goes we will leave here forever.'

She made a move to push herself from her seat and Garrick immediately put his hands on either side of her waist and lifted her easily to her feet. Then he supported her as she crossed the room to drop down beside her grandmother. It was going to be a joy having him there to assist her. For the first time since the accident she no longer felt disadvantaged by her injury.

'Grandmama, I'm relieved that we can be open with each other about this. As long as we continue to pretend we don't know in front of him, it will be so much easier for us to bear what's coming.'

'He insists the house must be made festive for your nuptials and to celebrate the Lord's name day, of course. I've already got Bates searching out the necessary items from the attics and the maids and footmen appear to be happy to take care of this onerous task for us.'

Garrick cleared his throat indicating he wished to speak. 'Is there a tenant already selected to take over this place when we go?'

'I wish there were, my lord, but staff will talk. We have to pay double wages in order to keep anyone here because of the unwanted occupants we share the place with. Thomas has made every effort to find someone suitable but nobody wishes to live here despite the fact this place is in excellent repair and would make anyone a healthy profit from the farms on the estate.'

'If you would permit me, my lady, I will take care of this. I have exactly the family in mind who will relish the thought of having ghostly neighbours.'

'Then please do so. That is one less thing to worry about. You will be shocked to hear my granddaughter refused to have bride clothes made and now it is too late to set anything in motion.'

'I have more than enough ensembles, and all in the first stare of fashion, and to make more would be a shocking waste of money.'

He looked at her with approval. 'I'm delighted to hear you say so, my dear. Not that I am likely to be consulted on such matters as you've already pointed out to me you're in a position to buy as many gowns as you require without asking my permission.'

Her grandmother was surprised to hear that they had discussed such things after so short an acquaintance. 'I can assure you, my lord, that your future wife spends her money wisely. She supports many charities and there are dozens of families in the neighbourhood that have successful businesses because of her investment in their skills.'

* * *

Eloise wanted to supervise her move upstairs. 'I'm not sure if it will be more dangerous for you to come with me or for you to remain here.'

'We agreed it was safer for us to be together.' Again, he supported her with his arm as they made their long trek from the small drawing room to her domain.

As they approached, the door swung open of its own volition. His hair stood on end. His fingers tightened around her waist and she squeezed his hand.

'It's a good sign that Brother Francis

has returned to his post. He was missing when I left earlier.'

Something flickered almost out of his vision. 'I saw him, at least I think I did. He's dressed in a monk's habit but it's not brown, it's grey.'

She didn't reply to him but spoke to the ghost. 'This is my future husband, Viscount Forsyth, I forbid you to harm him in any way.'

If the spectre replied he heard nothing. He considered himself a sensible fellow, not frightened of anything, but his skin crawled as he walked deeper into her apartment.

'There's something I need to ask you, Garrick, I wish to bring my personal staff with me. I want no one else to serve me.'

'I want you to be happy and will do everything in my power to make this happen. Bring whoever you want. No doubt you will wish to bring your gelding too.'

'Naturally, I trust him with my life. I expect you disapprove of the fact that I was riding astride — my injured leg makes riding side-saddle impossible for me.'

'As long as you remain within the park then I have no objection. Do you drive?'

'I do, but nothing more exciting than a gig. Could I persuade you to buy me a high-perch phaeton for my wedding gift?'

Despite his unease in his surroundings he chuckled. 'Over my dead body, young lady. However, I shall purchase one for myself and you may sit beside me on the box.'

She pulled a face. 'Then that will have to do. Why did you ask if I could handle the reins?'

They were now in what was obviously her bedchamber. It was a gloomy place, the windows little more than slits set in the thick walls and they let in almost no light.

'I was thinking that if you cannot ride in public you could drive instead. It's no more than half an hour to the nearest village and an hour to the town.

I'm certain you'll wish to visit both.'

'I thought you would insist I travel in a closed carriage. I'm finding you a most surprising gentleman and not at all what I expected from an aristocrat.'

He was about to answer when something hit him between the shoulder blades. He was propelled forward at such speed he lost his footing and fell headlong. It was pure luck that his head missed hitting the wall.

She was down beside him before he had recovered his wits. 'Lie still,' she whispered, 'pretend you're dead. I cannot keep you safe if you don't.'

He didn't argue. She must have some plan in mind. If being with her couldn't keep him safe then he'd have to insist they moved at once to Penston.

His heart was hammering, but he forced his limbs to remain still. There was a malevolent presence hovering over him.

'Brother James, what have you done? You were a man of God, spent your days doing good for the sick and needy.

How can you now be a murderer?'

There was a pause in which he thought the ghost was speaking. Then she replied.

'You are no friend of mine. You and your companions will remove yourself from my presence. I shall not communicate with you again.'

The weight that appeared to have been holding him to the floor vanished. He rolled and regained his feet.

'What did he say to you?'

'He swore he would remove the obstacle from his path one way or another. You heard me send them away and he was forced to go. The crucifix you wear should have been protection against them. You should never have come — I should never have agreed to this arranged marriage.'

'We must leave here, all of us, immediately and leave this place to them. I'm the last in my line, I cannot risk my life by remaining here however much I might wish to.'

'My grandfather is too sick to travel

even so short a distance. You must go home, Garrick, but I'll remain here until the end.'

He had intended to agree but said something else entirely. 'I shall remove myself to the nearest hostelry — presumably they cannot follow me there. We can meet each day until we marry.'

Her face lit up. Her remarkable eyes sparkled like gemstones. 'There's a substantial property no more than half a mile from here — it's within the grounds of the Priory and was occupied by visiting dignitaries. As far as I know it is habitable still. You can move there. They cannot leave this building so you will be safe.'

'I still think it would be better for you to move into the main part of the house — these cloisters are dismal and I cannot understand why you wish to live here.' She frowned but he raised a hand to prevent her from protesting. 'I'm well aware that you chose these rooms because of your infirmity. As you cannot climb stairs then you must all come with me. I'm certain Sir Thomas can move so short a distance without making his condition worse.'

For a moment she was undecided then she nodded vigorously. 'That's a perfect notion. When I explain it to them I'm certain they'll agree that it's the only possible solution to this problem.'

Her maid, a plump woman of middle years and smiling countenance, appeared in the door. 'Polly, I was about to send for you. The company has twice attempted to murder his lordship so we must move to the guest house in the grounds. Kindly have all my belongings packed and transferred there.'

The astonishment on the poor woman's face was comical.

'No, Polly dearest, do not look so scandalised. Sir Thomas and her ladyship will accompany us. I'm going to speak to them now. There's still an hour or two of daylight and I wish to be safely installed in my new abode before dark.'

★ ★ ★

By evening the entire household had transferred, hopefully leaving the unwanted intruders behind. The house had a dozen bedchambers, plus half a dozen usable rooms on the nursery floor and further rooms in the attics that were quite serviceable.

Dinner had been delayed in order to allow the kitchen staff to get the range burning and transfer the contents of the store rooms. Garrick had been closeted with her grandfather since they arrived but now they were coming to join them in the delightful drawing room before they finally dined.

'Grandmama, I can't think why we didn't move here years ago. Despite the fact that the place has been empty and no fires lit this winter, already it's warmer than the Priory.'

'The only disadvantage, my love, is that we can no longer accommodate so many guests for your wedding and for the Christmas festivities.'

'I think half the people you invited can drive here quite easily and there's ample room for those that live more than an hour away. Thank goodness you had the foresight to have the place cleaned and repaired regularly.'

'You know, this space seems more like home than the Priory ever did even though I have spent more than sixty years in that place. Your grandpapa is delighted to be here, are you not, my dear?'

'I am, Emma, we shall have an excellent time living here. I shall do better away from the worry of what lurks in the stonework of my ancestral home.'

His colour was better and he was walking more briskly. Was it possible living with the ghosts had been aggravating his condition?

Garrick offered his hand and she took it. 'Thank God you had this place we could all transfer to. It's more than adequate for our needs. The only drawback, as far as Sir Thomas and I can see, is that we'll have to return to use the chapel for the ceremony.'

'I can't see a difficulty doing that, after all it's the Lord's house and they cannot enter there.'

The butler was the only one put out by this lowering of standards. He bowed stiffly when he announced dinner and did not greet them by name as he usually did.

She walked in on Garrick's arm, well satisfied with the day's events. He looked magnificent in his evening black; she could not believe her luck that the gentleman who had been chosen for her was not only personable, but also kind, intelligent and broad-minded.

'That ensemble is quite stunning, Eloise. Why am I not surprised your gown isn't of the accepted colour for unmarried young ladies?'

The shimmering sparkles ran through her fingers. 'The underskirt is cream, only this is emerald.'

'I have been derelict in my duties as I have yet to give you a betrothal ring. After dinner perhaps we can go somewhere quiet and I can do it then.'

'We shall have this chamber to ourselves after dinner as my grandparents always retire immediately after they've eaten. As we're dining so late tonight I'm sure they'll wish to go immediately after the meal's finished.'

The food was excellent, as always, and as she'd predicted they walked alone into the drawing room afterwards. The room was wonderfully warm; not something she was used to. She sat on the daybed but for some reason he didn't join her.

He remained on his feet in front of her until she was settled and then dropped to one knee and took her hands in his.

'Miss Granville, will you do me the inestimable honour of becoming my wife? Make me the happiest of men.'

Her first inclination had been to laugh at his nonsense but his expression was serious, his eyes not laughing. She sat up straighter before replying.

'Thank you for your offer, my lord, I am delighted to accept.'

He raised her hands to his mouth and kissed each knuckle in turn. A wave of unexpected heat surged around her and she tried to pull them away. His fingers tightened and for a second there was a silent struggle before she acquiesced.

Still holding one hand firmly he released the other and dipped into his waistcoat pocket to remove a small leather ring box fastened with gold filigree. He flicked it open and revealed the ring.

'It's beautiful. How did you know to choose an emerald?'

He surged to his feet in one smooth movement and then took the seat beside her. He removed the ring and immediately she held out her hand for him to push it over her knuckle. Not only did it exactly match her eyes, it was also a perfect fit.

'This is a family heirloom, my love, it was my mama's before you. This is another sign that we're meant to be together.'

Before she could protest he had gathered her close, tilted her face towards him and then his lips were pressed against hers. For a second she stiffened but then the sensation was so pleasurable she relaxed and began to enjoy her first kiss.

It ended too soon. 'There, the matter's settled. Neither of us can renege as it is unconscionable for a gentleman to kiss a young lady to whom he's not betrothed. Your reputation would be in tatters, as would mine, if we do not marry as planned in two weeks' time.'

She rested her hot cheeks against his shoulder, loving the feel of the fabric on her skin. She sighed. 'How can we be so happy together when we only met this morning?'

'If you had been listening, miss, you would have heard me say that our stars are aligned and it has always been written that we should be together.'

She drew back so she could see him. Something made her reach out and touch his face. His skin was rough beneath her fingertips. His expression changed and a strange darkness clouded his eyes and a flush appeared along his cheekbones.

Abruptly he removed her hand and moved to the far end of the seat. Had she offended him by her wanton behaviour? He understood that she was concerned.

'No, sweetheart, you did nothing wrong. I gave my word to Sir Thomas that I would not share your bed until we returned to Penston and were married the second time in front of the earl. I shall not be able to keep my promise if you touch me like that.'

5

Garrick cursed inwardly that he'd forgotten for a moment his future bride was scarcely out of the schoolroom. Having no mother to speak to her about such intimate matters, he doubted she had any concept of what happened between a man and his wife in the bedroom. He must keep his distance until he knew her well enough to explain, to reassure her that nothing was going to take place that she didn't wish to participate in.

'I'll carry you to your bedchamber, my love, and then I have letters to write. Shall we ride together in the morning?'

'I should like that above anything. We have three horses up to your weight — do you wish me to send word to the stables or will you go yourself and choose?'

He stopped outside her door. Her maid appeared and smiled approvingly as he set Eloise on her feet.

'I'll go first thing to make my choice. Good night, I hope tomorrow's not as eventful.'

'I doubt there's a couple in Christendom that has spent the day as we just did.' She held up her hand and counted on her fingers. 'One, a first meeting. Two, an attack by ghosts. Three, a decision to share an apartment without the benefit of clergy. Four, a second attack. Five, removal of an entire household to a new abode. Six, a formal proposal and celebratory dinner. I am quite exhausted just reciting the list.'

'Do you prefer to ride before or after breakfast?'

'I eat at eight o'clock then ride for an hour or two. I always take luncheon. This is served at midday and although gentlemen do not prefer to eat then, you're most welcome to join my grandmother and me. Good night, Garrick, I cannot tell you how glad I am to have you here.'

He strolled back to his own rooms and sat down to write two letters. The first would be sent by express to his grandfather explaining that in the circumstances he could not possibly leave until after the demise of his host. Of the ghosts, he mentioned nothing at all — the fewer people knew about them, the better. Although Grandfather had actually mentioned to him the Priory was haunted.

A second letter would be sent to his factor. This man had earned the opportunity to take over an estate and run it for his own benefit. He had taken care of Penston with loyalty and dedication for the past twenty years. The fact that he had mentioned on more than one occasion that he had an interest in the supernatural would make him an ideal occupant for the haunted Priory. If anyone could tame these unpleasant spirits it was he.

Eventually he stripped and tumbled into bed, not bothering to put on his nightshirt. Usually he wore one when staying away from home but tonight he was too tired to bother with such niceties. Foster had instructions to bring his shaving water at seven o'clock.

He had not expected to sleep so soundly but did not rouse until his valet started banging about in the dressing room. For a moment he was disorientated, not sure exactly where he was. Then he yawned, smiled and stretched.

There was a third letter to be written before he broke his fast. This was to the physician who was taking care of his grandfather. The man had mentioned knowing an expert in the field of broken bones who had worked miracles even for those whose injury was several years old.

If Eloise was prepared to endure such an agonising procedure then he would support her wholeheartedly. Equally, if she decided against it he would be even happier. As far as he was concerned it made no difference to him whether she had a limp or not, but he believed he knew her well enough to understand that being able to move about the place freely was incentive enough for her to wish to have her leg reset.

Of course, it was possible she would not be a suitable candidate. Nevertheless, it made sense to set things in motion so when they finally returned to his home she could be seen immediately.

'You won't be riding today, my lord, unless you want to be knee-deep in snow,' Foster told him.

'Devil take it! It must have been snowing heavily all night for there to be so much. I thought it scarcely cold enough for snow.'

'It's bitterly cold out there now, sir, no one will be going anywhere until it thaws. It's a blizzard outside and looks set in for a few days at least.'

'I have three letters to go — they'll have to wait as will my ride. Is your accommodation satisfactory?'

'Very, my lord. The upper servants have rooms downstairs and a private parlour. The housekeeper and butler also reside in this apartment. The others are somewhere in the attic.' He grinned. 'The maids are on one side of the house and the footmen on the other. There'll be no misbehaviour under this roof.'

'I'm glad to hear it. The stables attached to this establishment didn't look large enough to accommodate all the horses. When the snow is clear I'll have to walk to the Priory in order to find a mount.'

'Don't you worry about that, I'll make sure a suitable animal is fetched here for you. Miss Granville's gelding's already *in situ*.'

'As long as our team is well looked after, I care not where they're stabled. I wonder if they have a sleigh and suitably robust horses to pull it?' He was speaking out loud and didn't require an answer. 'I'll go down and check. If there is one it's unlikely to be housed here. The outside-men can be set to clearing the drive from here to the Priory — I'll ask Sir Thomas if he's happy for me to put things in motion.'

Foster knew when he was expected to speak and when he must remain silent. His man had been with him for five years and Garrick would be lost without him.

He knocked on Eloise's sitting room door and Polly opened it with a smile. 'Miss Eloise is ready to go down and is waiting for you, my lord.'

He moved towards her. 'Good morning, I fear we'll not be able to ride today or indeed for several days.'

'I'm not overfond of snow; nasty, cold, white stuff, but I own it makes the park look beautiful.'

He reached down and lifted her into his arms. She settled as if she belonged there — which, of course, she did. 'Does Sir Thomas have a sleigh for such weather?'

'I am before you on that score, Garrick, I've already sent Tom to fetch it. The snow's no longer falling hard so once the drive is clear we'll be able to get out. There are two such vehicles

— one for conveying passengers and the other for heavy goods.'

'Then later this morning shall we go out together and admire the winter scene? This house is a sensible size unlike the Priory or Penston Hall. I cannot remember being warm in the winter before. I think when I'm the earl I'll have built for us a modern residence of a similar size to this.'

'I should like that above anything. Then there would be no danger of ghosts.'

'Are you suggesting the monks might be able to follow you?'

'No, but I've a nasty suspicion wherever there might be spirits they'll be able to communicate with me.'

He placed her on the boards then put his arm around her waist so he could support her as she walked. 'There's no need for me to enquire the whereabouts of the breakfast parlour as there's an appetising aroma drifting from that passageway.'

* * *

Her grandparents never breakfasted with her — they ate in their own apartments. It would be pleasant to share this meal with another person and someone she was coming to like very much.

'Sit down, Eloise, and I'll serve us both.'

He guided her to a chair and swivelled it round so she could sit without difficulty. 'I like bacon, any sort of eggs as well as several slices of toasted bread. The marmalade and conserve are always waiting on the table. I prefer coffee. What would you like to drink?'

His smile made her pulse skip. 'Another thing we have in common.'

Whilst he busied himself at the buffet she had time to look at him without fear he would catch her staring. His topcoat was dark blue, his unmentionables hugged his thighs in such a way she thought they might be made of calfskin. His hessians were immaculate and fitted his lower limbs so closely she imagined his valet would have difficulty removing them.

90

'Do you like what you see, sweet-heart?' His amused enquiry made her drop her cutlery.

'How did you know I was looking at you? Do you have mysterious powers that allow you to see through the back of your head?'

He turned and brought two piled plates to the table. 'I guessed you might be taking an interest in my appearance and your reply confirmed it.'

Once they both had a cup of the dark, bitter brew they both preferred, he returned to the subject. She wished he had not.

'Do I come up to snuff? Are you satisfied with your bargain?'

'Fishing for compliments, my lord? We both know that you're a handsome man with a good physique. Not that it makes any difference to our arrange-ment: if you were bracket-faced, with spindly limbs and a crooked nose, I should still be obliged to marry you.' No sooner had she spoken the words than she realised he was the one who had been stuck with a cripple.

Her appetite had deserted her. She pushed herself to her feet and was going to leave but he was too quick for her. Gently he pressed on her shoulders until she subsided into the chair.

'No, whatever you might think to the contrary, Eloise, I am delighted with the arrangement. Devil take it, child! You have a damaged leg but the rest of you is perfect.'

He had resumed his seat beside her but for some reason she ignored his compliment and concentrated on his assertion that she was a child.

'I shall be eighteen years of age in January; many young ladies are already married by then. How dare you insinuate I'm immature.'

Instead of taking offence at her reprimand he laughed. 'I'm eight years your senior. To me you're still too young to take on the responsibilities of a countess.'

She was about to argue, to tell him she'd been running the Priory for her grandmother these past two years, but then recalled that he'd kissed her — and mentioned his desire to share her bed.

'In which case, my lord, I think it best if our marriage remains in name alone until I reach my majority. I cannot think that the liberties you took with my person were appropriate in the circumstances, as you state that you regard me as a child.'

There was an ominous silence. She had overstepped the mark. Too late to repine. The damage was done and, unlike other young ladies, she could not flee but must remain where she was whilst she got her comeuppance.

'*Touché!* You may relax, Eloise, I've not taken offence at your impertinence.' He placed his hand over hers. 'I accept your insistence that you're a woman grown and quite ready to become my true wife when we marry. The fact that I shall be breaking my solemn vow to both your grandfather and mine is a mere bagatelle.'

He was deliberately goading her. It would have been better if she'd held her tongue but the words that came tumbling out of her mouth were quite scandalous.

'In which case, I shall expect you to come to me tonight. After all, if we're to marry in three weeks' time I hardly think it matters.'

He choked on his drink and sprayed the table with coffee. She hammered on his back whilst he continued to splutter. 'I beg your pardon, Garrick, that was unpardonable. I just wished to shock you, not ruin your breakfast.'

Eventually he recovered his breath, stood up and marched from the room without saying a single word. She wasn't sure if she was relieved or dismayed by his behaviour. Normally she was a well-behaved, sensible young lady yet, in the space of twenty-four hours, her entire character appeared to have changed — and not for the better either.

There was little point in her going after him as with his long legs he could be anywhere by now. She would just have to wait until he had regained his temper and then attempt to apologise a second time. She continued to eat her breakfast and was halfway through a slice of toasted bread when an appalling thought occurred to her.

What if he took her at her word? She wasn't ready to discover the intimacies of married life even if he did make her heart beat faster. There was no question of allowing him into her bedchamber until they had known each other longer than a day or two.

Disconsolately she abandoned her half-eaten meal and wandered slowly to the orangery which adjoined the side of the house. This was heated by a complicated arrangement of pipes which ran under the floor. Although no exotic plants or flowers grew here now it was still a delightful place to sit and view the winter landscape outside the walls of glass.

She'd not been there above a quarter of an hour when he suddenly spoke from right behind her. Her bladder almost emptied. 'I'm in two minds whether to take you at your word or turn you across my knee.'

As she was braced against the window shelf she was able to turn without losing her balance. He was no more than a few inches from her. 'If you're foolish enough to attempt either option I promise that you'll live to regret it.'

It was difficult maintaining her dignity when a solid wall of exceedingly male flesh was no more than a hand's breadth from her face. Her pulse was erratic. She dare not raise her head to meet his eyes.

She took three calming breaths and then filled the silence. 'I think it most ungentlemanly of you to creep about the place and startle a person half to death.'

His voice was soft when he finally answered. 'Are there any other insults you'd like to throw at my head? I can assure you I'm eager to hear them.'

She drew breath to answer but then considered this might be a rhetorical question and remained quiet. He was so close she was warmed by his heat. His breath brushed across the top of her head, almost giving her palpitations.

'Please, I'm sorry, but you make me so nervous I find myself talking nonsense. Can I go now?' Even to her own ears she sounded like a terrified child, which just served to confirm the opinion he'd expressed earlier and that she had objected to so strenuously.

His answer was to put his arms around her and draw her to him so every inch of her overheated body was touching him. 'Now, little one, do you understand my problem? One moment you're a desirable, passionate woman; the next, a babbling child. However much I might wish to, I won't be making love to you tonight or any night this year.'

'And the other threat?' Her voice was muffled because her head was resting against his shirt front.

'The spanking that I threatened? I don't believe in physical chastisement for children or for wives — or in your case, future wife. I hope that reassures you.'

'We need to talk . . . '

'Is that not what we've been doing this past ten minutes?'

'Don't try to aggravate me, sir, you know exactly to what I refer. We know so little about each other and we should remedy that situation immediately.'

There was a wooden settle conveniently placed nearby and they sat together. 'Shall I go first?' He nodded. 'My name day is the twenty-fifth of January. I cannot abide to eat fish of any description but am very fond of meat. I don't drink alcohol — not because I dislike it but because my grandparents disapprove. I love to read and discuss matters of a political nature often though this is best left to gentlemen, I've no interest whatsoever in fashion, and am an indifferent seamstress.'

'I drink, but not to excess, I like a wager or two, but again in moderation. I eat anything apart from food smothered with rich cream sauces. I've been running the family estates for the past year as my grandfather's health deteriorated. I toured most of Europe in the years between leaving school and attending university. I prefer the country to the town.' He had crossed his legs at the ankle and her eyes were drawn to the length of his limbs as they had been before.

'I forgot — I can sing and play the pianoforte but cannot paint a watercolour to save my life.'

'I played the violin as a boy. Is there a music room here? I doubt any piano will be tuned but I think I can make a reasonable attempt to do so as I've seen it done several times.'

Without conscious thought she had been leaning against him and his arm was around her shoulders ensuring that she didn't slip. 'I've only been here once before myself so have no idea how many reception rooms there are, or if one of them might be for music. Shall we go and investigate?'

The orangery faced towards the

extensive woodland and from there the narrow drive that led to the Priory was not visible.

'I wonder how long it will take to clear a path so we can access the stables,' he said as they made their way around the house looking for a music room — or at least a chamber with musical instruments they could use.

'We have a surfeit of outside servants in the winter as there is little they can do to maintain the fabric of the buildings, or the grounds and gardens. I'm certain both sledges will be here later today.'

The search was fruitless so they retreated to the small drawing room where her grandmother was now situated. Grandpapa was conserving his strength and remaining in bed until dinner time.

The next few days were spent in similar fashion. She and Garrick played Loo, Whist and even resorted to several riotous rounds of spillikins and whilst doing so, she got to know him better. They read, laughed and even sang together as well as taking several enjoyable drives in the sledge.

The ghosts were a thing of the past and she was able to push their behaviour to the back of her mind and enjoy his company. Occasionally she ventured with him into the orangery where the servants who were not engaged on other tasks were happily constructing garlands, wreaths and bows with which to decorate the house in the days leading up to the arrival of the first guests. Those unable to make the return journey without overnighting with them were expected to come at the beginning of next week. She was eagerly anticipating the beginning of the festivities to celebrate her marriage and the Lord's name day.

6

Garrick decided it would make sense for him to examine the property he would be in control of next year. His stay at the Priory had been so brief he had had no time to make any judgements. From the exterior it appeared well maintained but it was quite possible the dozen or so rooms that were housed in the magnificent ancient arch might be in disrepair as they'd not been in use.

This building, like the guest house, was separate from the Priory itself. He wouldn't venture into the main building again unless he had Eloise with him. He should be safe anywhere that wasn't physically attached to where the ghosts resided.

The gelding he'd been allocated was adequate, but no more than that. He wouldn't trust it over large fences so in one way was relieved the snow had yet to thaw. His coachman greeted him with less enthusiasm than usual.

'My lord, I ain't one to complain, but mighty strange goings-on there's been around here. If it weren't for the snow I reckon young Bobby would've taken off.'

Bobby was the under-coachman. 'Tell me what's been happening.'

'Well, my lord, I can't rightly say but there's been noises in the night, things banging about in the Priory and no one living there. The other grooms say this place is haunted and I reckon they're right.'

'It's the reason we removed to the guest house — the story that the roof had sprung several leaks was a false-hood. Until I came here I believed such stories to be superstitious nonsense but now I know different.'

'As long as they stay put, I ain't worried. But I'll be glad to leave here, that's for sure.'

'There will be at least a dozen extra

horses arriving in a day or two. Put Bobby in charge of our team and you help out with the new animals. Stable my mount somewhere warm; I'm going to investigate the gatehouse.'

There was no necessity for him to explain his movements to his servant but having just discussed the fact that there were ghosts living — if that was what they did — in the Priory had put them on a different footing.

He had obtained the keys to the doors from the butler and was able to let himself in with no difficulty. The place was icy, frost patterned the inside of the windows. His breath steamed in front of him and he was glad of his thick greatcoat, gloves and beaver.

Like the Priory itself, this place had been kept in good repair. It was unfurnished, but the lime-washed walls and leaded windows were intact. This had originally been the accommodation for visiting clerics so was without a large entrance hall or spacious reception rooms.

On the first floor there were a dozen or more modest bedchambers which would be ideal for upper servants. He had seen enough. As he turned to leave, the door behind him slammed shut of its own volition. Something icy began to squeeze his chest. Invisible hands were attempting to drain the life from him. How could this be? Were there a second set of spectres living here or had the monks managed to migrate across the inner courtyard?

He recited the Lord's Prayer out loud whilst he forced his unwilling limbs to respond to his command. He managed to raise his right hand and press it against the heavy weight of the gold crucifix. The pressure on his chest vanished and he was able to breathe freely again.

He staggered to the door, his breath rasping in his throat, desperate to remove himself from the danger that stalked these corridors. Only by clinging onto the rope that served as a banister did he remain upright as he hurtled down the narrow staircase. The hair on the back of his neck stood up. They were following him. He was surrounded by malevolent spirits.

'Our Father which art in heaven, hallowed be thy name,' he shouted at the top of his voice in the hope this would keep them at bay long enough for him to reach the exit. The door was closed and he'd been certain he'd left it open.

His heart was pounding, his breathing becoming difficult again. He flung himself headfirst at the closed door. It wouldn't open. He continued to recite the prayer but it was becoming increasingly hard to continue.

His knees buckled and his head fell forward and slammed painfully against the iron hinges. Then the door was flung open and he fell into the arms of his groom.

'Get me out, lock the door behind me,' was all he managed to whisper before losing consciousness.

He came around to find himself stretched out on a bed of straw in an empty stable. His man was kneeling at his side.

'You stay put, my lord, I sent Bobby for the sledge. You've a nasty gash on your forehead from where you fell. I reckon you've got the concussion as well.'

'Is the door to the gatehouse locked?'

'It is, right and tight. There's something nasty living in there, sure enough. We never saw nothing but I felt it when I dragged you out.'

Garrick was finding it easier to breathe. There was a makeshift bandage around his head and he raised his hand to touch it. It came away stained red. He needed sutures in the injury. He hoped there was someone living here who could do this as no physician could be fetched with the snow so deep.

One thing was certain: his grandfather would never have arranged this union with Eloise if he'd known the true state of affairs at the Priory.

★ ★ ★

Eloise was admiring the garlands that had been stretched out across the floor in the orangery when a footman rushed in.

'Miss Eloise, his lordship has had an accident at the Priory and they are bringing him back on the sledge. He will require stitches in his wound.'

For a moment she was unable to comprehend what she'd just been told. Then her head cleared and she took charge.

'He's too large to convey upstairs to his apartment without mishap so we must prepare a place to put him in one of the smaller reception rooms.'

In her search for a music room she'd discovered several small chambers and, if she remembered correctly, one of them already had a daybed of sufficient length to accommodate him. She pushed aside her fears and concentrated on the task in hand.

Until that moment she had been unaware Garrick had gone out and she swallowed a lump in her throat. Bates, the housekeeper, arrived at her side.

'They are preparing what I'll need, miss, and I have instructed for them to be brought here to this chamber. I've stitched up many cuts and gashes over the past years but never treated anyone but servants and outside-men.'

'His lordship will be pleased you're experienced in this matter. If you weren't, Polly would have had to sew him together.' This sounded so ridiculous they both smiled.

'The message from the stables said his lordship had stumbled in the snow and hit his head. He's not comatose so I don't think it can be anything too serious.'

'I can hear the sledge pulling up outside.' Eloise gestured for the housekeeper to go. 'I'll remain here — please assist in any way you can.'

Two maids were busy putting the linen on the daybed and a footman was rearranging the furniture to her satisfaction. A side table had been placed adjacent to the *chaise longue* ready for the items the housekeeper would need.

'Bring a jug of watered wine — make sure that it's warm.' The footman nodded and went to fetch what she'd asked for.

At times like this she felt her infirmity the most. She should be beside her future husband, holding his hand and comforting him, but even something as mundane as that was beyond her capabilities.

There wasn't long to wait before she heard shuffling footsteps approaching the open door. She had expected to see Garrick brought in on a hurdle but instead he appeared on his own feet. He was ably supported by his two grooms. His face was blood-streaked, the bandage around his head sodden with his gore, but he smiled at her.

'Don't look so perturbed, my dear, I've lost a lot of blood but once this damned cut is sewn up I'll be absolutely splendid.'

'My housekeeper will do that for you. Your valet is coming with your night-shirt . . . '

'Good God! I've no intention of remaining here and certainly not of removing my garments.'

His vehemence reassured her that he was indeed in no danger. 'You will be more comfortable without your great-coat — would you consent to take that off at least?'

She stood to one side whilst his man, with the help of one of the grooms, expertly removed not only Garrick's greatcoat but his jacket and cravat as well. Next his boots were pulled off and he was settled on top of the coverlet. The room was pleasantly warm as she'd fortuitously arranged for every fire in the house to be lit until the new year.

The housekeeper bustled in followed by a maid carrying the necessary items. Eloise took her position behind the patient's head so she could lean against the end of the daybed and still be able to rest her hand on his shoulders if necessary.

He looked remarkably relaxed for a man who was about to be sewn up like a piece of material. She wasn't squeamish but was forced to grip tight to the daybed as the bandages were removed.

The housekeeper had a pad of clean cloth ready in her hand. 'My lord, could I ask you to press this over the wound? It will stop the blood from flowing whilst I stitch.'

Eloise wasn't sure how this was going to work as the pad would cover the injury thus making it impossible for stitches to be put in. Her worry was unnecessary as Garrick appeared to understand exactly what he was to do.

Within a remarkably short space of time four sutures had been securely placed, a fresh bandage applied and his face wiped clean.

'Thank you, you're obviously an expert.'

The housekeeper curtsied and with a

flick of her skirts vanished, followed by the maid carrying the tray. His valet had already poured a large pewter mug of the watered wine and handed it to his master.

'You must drink all of it, Garrick, in order to replace the blood you've lost,' she told him sternly. He started to rise but she put her hands on his shoulders and pushed him down. 'No, remain where you are at least for an hour or two.'

She manoeuvred herself around so she could sit on the end of the daybed. Without a second thought she lifted his stockinged feet and placed them in her lap. Then she gestured that his man should leave so they could be alone.

'Now, tell me how you came to be injured.'

She listened to his dreadful story and was appalled. 'We must pray that they cannot find their way here. If there is the remotest possibility we shall have to cancel the house party.'

He drained the last of the wine,

replaced the mug on the side table and leaned forward, his expression serious. 'I was wondering if there might be underground passages linking the two buildings — if so, that would explain how they came to be in the gatehouse.'

'There are, I'd quite forgotten. I'm certain there are none that come out this far so we'll be safe enough here.'

'I cannot in all conscience allow anyone to move into the Priory at the moment. It would be far too dangerous.'

'You can hardly expect the new tenant to live here, so far away from the stables and coach house. I sincerely wish you had never come, Garrick, and that instead we'd come to you.'

His smile was rueful. 'As do I, my love, but I am here and we must make the best of it. I think we'd better speak to your grandparents, explain exactly what has transpired, and persuade them to leave here immediately after Christmas.'

'Grandpapa's health has been failing

rapidly, I'm not certain he would survive the journey. Anyway, he wishes to die here and be buried in the family mausoleum.'

He sighed and leaned back. His eyes closed and she thought he'd drifted off to sleep. She would leave him to rest and go and seek out her relatives — word would have reached them and they would be anxious.

'No, sweetheart, remain where you are. I was gathering my thoughts, not sleeping.'

She settled back, loving the heavy weight of his legs across her lap. It took all her self-control not to explore the contours of his feet and calves with her fingers. What she felt for him could not possibly be love, but he stirred her senses in a most delightful way.

'The banns were called last Sunday so we could be married in ten days' time. Would you be agreeable to bringing the ceremony forward?'

'I'm prepared to do anything that will keep you safe. Are you thinking that once the knot is tied they will give up their pursuit?'

'It's a possibility. I fear they might start attacking the grooms and outside-men who reside close to the Priory.'

'I'll go back and try and speak to them . . .'

He moved so fast she had no time to reprimand him for grabbing her arms so firmly. 'You'll do no such thing, Eloise. Do I make myself quite clear?'

He was no more than a few inches from her; she should have been frightened by his anger but the opposite was true. His violent reaction was because he wished to keep her safe and she couldn't fault him for that.

Instead of struggling, of complaining at his firm grip, she relaxed and leaned into his embrace. What happened next was inevitable. He swung his legs aside just long enough to lift her onto his lap and then replaced them on the daybed.

Before she realised what was happening she was stretched out beside him being thoroughly kissed. He made her feel perfect, like other young ladies and not somehow inferior because of her injury.

How things might have ended she had no idea as she was just following his lead. Then she was rudely tipped onto the floor and landed ignominiously on her derriere.

'Go away, Eloise, every time I kiss you I find my resolve slipping away.'

It was all very well for him to dismiss her so cavalierly but getting to her feet was no easy task. Then his arm came down, slid around her waist and hoisted her upright as if she weighed no more than a bag of feathers.

'It would serve you right, my lord, if your stitches came apart and you had to undergo the procedure a second time.'

He had rolled so his back was to her and she heard him chuckle. She viewed him with disfavour for a moment and then smiled. She waited until she was by the door so even if he wanted to he could not reach her before she escaped.

'I have decided, Garrick, that not

only will I marry you in ten days' time, I will also become your true wife. I've read in one of the ancient books in the library here that only a pure maiden can communicate with beings from the other side.'

She was out of the door and had closed it firmly behind her before he had the opportunity to reply. From the way he reacted whenever she was in his arms, she doubted it would be too difficult to make him forget his vow.

★ ★ ★

Garrick was tempted to go after her but it would be an unfair contest. He wished for her sake that she could move as freely as he could. What bee had got into her bonnet to make her offer such an ultimatum? Apart from a dull ache where he had struck his head, he was fully recovered and had no intention of lingering where he was a moment longer.

He looked around for his boots and

topcoat but they were nowhere in sight. His valet must have taken them away with him in the misguided notion that removing them would keep his master resting. The floors here were boards, not flagstones like the Priory, so it would be no hardship walking in his stockinged feet.

For good measure he drained the last mug of watered wine and feeling in good spirits he went in search of the library. He recalled it had been in the vicinity of the study which was at the rear of the building on the right-hand side.

On emerging from his temporary chamber, he took stock of his abrupt surroundings. The passageway was deserted, no sign of a lurking footman to ask for directions. He put out a hand to steady himself and realised he was a trifle bosky. The wine had not been as diluted as it should have been.

He made his way to the end of the passageway and then began to open doors in the hope of locating the missing library. He was laughing whilst he searched. He was the one who was missing, not the library.

The third door he pushed open was the one he wanted. There was a fire burning — how thoughtful of Eloise to have this lit so he could be warm. To his delight he saw a comfortable chair adjacent to the fire and he flopped into it. It would do no harm to rest until he felt more the thing. He stretched out his legs to the blaze and fell asleep.

7

Eloise was surprised, but delighted, to see that both her grandfather and grandmother were in the drawing room enjoying a mid-morning tray of freshly baked pastries and a jug of coffee.

'Come in, my dear girl, we were just talking about you,' Grandpapa said as he patted the space beside him on the sofa.

'You must be feeling better today, I can't remember the last time you joined us for refreshments at this time.'

His smile was warm. 'I do have more energy today. How is your young man? We heard he met with some sort of accident at the stables.'

She explained what had actually happened and reassured them that Garrick would be perfectly well apart from having stitches in his head. When she mentioned they intended to get

121

married as soon as it was legally possible the two exchanged glances.

'I think that would be wise, my love, as he can protect you better than I.'

'I know we have only known each other a short while but I'm certain we've spent more time together than most betrothed couples do before they are wed. I intend to share his bed . . . '

'Eloise, I've no wish to hear you speak of such things. How could you mention . . . ' Her grandmother was too shocked to continue. Grandpapa winked.

'I beg your pardon, forgive me for my indiscretion. Do I have your permission to speak to the housekeeper and have the wedding breakfast rearranged for the Monday after next? I shall also send word to the curate to be here to perform the ceremony.'

'My dear girl, I think it might be best if you were married in the village church and not the family chapel.'

There was no need for him to explain his reasoning — she knew the ghosts could invade this building as it was attached to the Priory itself.

Her grandmother had now recovered sufficiently to join in the conversation. 'I don't believe the banns were called there so without a licence the wedding cannot be held anywhere but the chapel.'

'I'd not thought of that, Grandmama. We must somehow obtain the licence.' She pushed herself clumsily to her feet. 'Excuse me, I shall speak to Garrick. He will know what to do.'

As she progressed slowly towards the room in which he was resting, she met his valet hurrying towards her. 'Miss Eloise, his lordship has vanished. I returned with a neckcloth, fresh jacket and clean boots and he was gone.'

'Have you searched anywhere?'

'No, miss, not as yet. It's not my place to do so without permission.'

'You have it — I'll enlist the help of our footmen. He cannot have gone far dressed as he is.'

The nearest door led into an anteroom and this held a bell-strap. She pulled it hard and waited impatiently for her summons to be answered.

'His lordship is missing. I wish you to search for him and get others to help. I shall return to the drawing room. You will inform me of your progress.'

Her grandparents did not seem unduly bothered by this event. 'He cannot have gone far, my dear girl, he will be found safe and well somewhere in the house. I'm certain nothing untoward has taken place this time.'

An hour later the house had been searched from top to bottom and Garrick was still not found. Now she was truly worried, as were her grandparents.

'The only explanation is that in the confusion from his injury he has ventured outside. Dressed as he was he will freeze to death if he's not located soon.'

'I thought you said he was perfectly lucid when you spoke to him, Eloise,' Grandpapa said.

'He was, which makes me terrified

that somehow he has been spirited away.'

'I'm sure you're worrying unnecessarily, there will be a perfectly rational explanation for his disappearance.'

'Grandmama, I pray that you're right. I wish I could search myself but it would take me too long.'

'Why don't you send for his two grooms? Get them and his valet to go from top to bottom of the house again. I'm sure one of them will locate him.'

'I'll do that.' She picked up the small brass bell that was kept on a side table for her personal use and rang it vigorously. The door flew open almost immediately. The footman nodded, bowed and retreated. There was nothing more she could do apart from worry.

The remainder of the day dragged past and Garrick had still not been located. Eventually, she decided she would have to look for herself, however long it took and however painful it was to limp up and down the long corridors.

Her grandparents had dined together

and then retired. The mood in the house was sombre. If nothing catastrophic had happened to him then why had he not appeared by now? The grooms and his valet had joined the outside search parties — they declined to come in until he'd been found. She refused to believe he'd perished in the snow. There must be another explanation.

She started in the room he'd been treated in then hobbled to the far end of the passageway and began to search systematically. Although the fires were lit every morning, the passageways were cold and the fires were allowed to go out overnight. The fourth door was the one to the library.

She pushed it open and held her candle high. The room was empty, just a faint glow from the dying fire to light it. As she turned to leave there was a slight sound and the hair on the back of her neck stood to attention.

Her heart was doing its best to escape from her bodice. Her legs were trembling. She moved a few feet into the room and listened. There it was again — the sound of heavy breathing. She crept forward and peered over the back of the armchair.

She was so shocked her fingers released their hold on the heavy candlestick and it fell, hitting Garrick on the head for a second time that day. His language made her ears burn.

'Devil take it! Have I not had sufficient injury?'

Naturally the candle had been snuffed out and she was unable to see anything at all. She was gripping for dear life to the back of the chair, unable to comprehend how he could have been so stupid as to sleep here all day whilst the entire household had been searching for him.

'We thought you taken by the ghosts, or outside freezing to death. Your men are still searching in the darkness. It will be entirely your fault if one of them perishes in your stead. I cannot believe you could do anything so stupid.'

He surged to his feet and towered over her. She didn't need to see his face to know he was irate. She could almost hear him grinding his teeth. She waited for him to reply but instead he strode past her as if she was invisible. The fact that he slammed the door was indication enough that she was better off without him.

Her eyes had now adjusted to the gloom and, by holding onto the arm of the chair, she was able to grope about on the carpet and recover both the candle and the candlestick. She pushed the candle into the embers and it lit, then she put it back where it belonged and was ready to depart.

How in heaven's name did none of the searchers see him sleeping in the chair? They must have merely opened the door, glanced around and then gone on. Why he had been asleep all day she had no idea and had no intention of enquiring until the morning, when he would hopefully have recovered his temper.

It would have been preferable to take the servants' staircase but this was too steep for her so she was obliged to make her way to the main staircase and begin her laborious ascent. She was a third of the way up when he bounded down.

'Let me help you, you've done enough walking today.'

She waited for him to put one arm under her legs and the other around her shoulders as he had done before, but to her horror he grabbed her about the knees and slung her over his shoulder like a sack of corn. He reversed his steps and bounded back to her apartment. The door to this was open and he walked in as if he had every right to be there.

All this done without a word being spoken on either side. He tipped her onto her daybed and then strode out. Despite the fact that he was obviously still furious with her, he had been kind enough to assist her on the stairs. To be transported about the place in such an undignified manner was no doubt part of her comeuppance for dropping a candlestick on his head and then calling him stupid.

In the time it had taken her to get halfway up the staircase he had returned to his chamber, changed his shirt, put on a fresh neckcloth, jacket and boots. How she envied him his ability to dash about the place like this. However hideous the procedure, she was determined to have her leg reset if it would give her the slightest chance of being more mobile.

Her eyes filled and she brushed away her tears. She was a veritable watering pot at the moment and it was all his fault. He was a most disruptive sort of gentleman. When he wasn't giving her palpitations, and sending heat flooding into most unexpected places, he was frightening her half to death with his anger.

★ ★ ★

Garrick found the search party easily enough as their torches flickered brightly in the darkness. He crunched through the snow waving his lantern until they came towards him. His men were most apologetic to have caused so much upset when in fact he had been safely sleeping in the library.

He returned to the house feeling a trifle foolish. If he hadn't imbibed so much wine he would not have passed out in the chair and slept for most of the day. He had fences to mend with Eloise as he had treated her poorly.

His valet had accompanied him and was there to take his outdoor garments when he stepped into the central hall. 'I shan't need you anymore tonight. Make sure you get into something dry and have a substantial meal.'

The mention of food made his stomach rumble. He'd eaten nothing since the night before and was sharp-set. He sent a footman to bring whatever was still available and told him he would be in the drawing room. With the shutters closed, the curtains drawn and the fire burning in both grates, the room was warm, almost too hot for comfort.

In his ancestral home he was used to food arriving cold because the kitchens were so far away from the dining room, and for all the chambers to be barely above freezing in the winter because they were so vast even the biggest fires could not keep them comfortable.

He settled in a padded armchair some distance from the fire and picked up a journal to peruse whilst he waited for his meal to arrive. Apart from the tug of the sutures in his scalp, he was fully recovered from his unpleasant experience.

The overmantel clock showed the time to be a little after seven. He would eat his supper and then go in search of Eloise, as she was unlikely to have retired so early.

He paused outside her sitting room and saw there was a sliver of golden light showing under the door. He knocked loudly and heard her call for him to enter. On opening the door, he saw her stretched out on the *chaise longue* with a rug over her legs. She put down her book and raised an eyebrow.

'Good evening, Eloise. Might I be permitted to join you?'

'As you are already inside I doubt that anything I say to the contrary will prevent you from coming further in.'

This was not an auspicious start. 'I owe you an apology for causing so much disruption and worry today.'

She waved towards a chair on the other side of the fire as if he were of no account. No one had ever had the temerity to treat him as if he were a servant. He took the seat without comment, knowing that if he spoke it would be to say something he might regret.

'I drank two pints of wine which had not been sufficiently diluted on an empty stomach and after a serious head injury. It's hardly surprising I behaved erratically and passed out in the library.'

'I cannot understand how you did not hear those who came in search of you.'

'And I cannot understand why those very people did not have the sense to search the room properly.'

'My footmen and your servants did a poor job indeed. I consider they got their just deserts for their shoddy work by being obliged to tramp about in the snow for several hours.'

'I'm sure you will be happy to know that none suffered from this experience. Now, there are more important matters we must discuss.'

When she put forward the idea that he send for a licence to allow them to marry in the parish church he was pleased to give her good news.

'The banns were read in the village as well as in your chapel, so we can marry there without the necessity of obtaining a licence to do so. The snow is several feet deep in places where the wind has caused it to drift. Will it be possible to get to the village?'

'As we have the sledge I can see no difficulty on that score. I doubt that any of our house guests will attempt the journey unless there's a thaw. Even those that live locally are likely to remain at home.'

'In the circumstances, the fewer strangers are here, the better. Servants gossip and you can be very sure everyone will be aware that St Cuthbert's Priory is haunted and that these ghosts are dangerous. I doubt any will remain once they hear that.'

'Then I'm glad it has snowed so heavily. For myself, I care not who comes to witness our wedding as long as my beloved grandparents are there. The house will be decorated in garlands and ribbons, there will be a yule log burning in the entrance hall — that is celebration enough for me.'

He leaned forward and she guessed what was coming. He watched her cheeks flood with colour and thought how enchanting she was when she was flustered.

'About your pronouncement, Eloise . . .'

'I made it up, I've not seen anything in any books about virgins and their ability to communicate with ghosts. I don't know what made me say such an outrageous thing.' She was looking down at her hands as she twisted them in her lap. She looked up and her magnificent eyes held him mesmerised.

'That's not strictly true. I do sincerely believe you'll be safer if I'm your real wife. I know you made a solemn promise to both our grandfathers but I think in the circumstances how we conduct our marriage is entirely our own business.'

'The reason I was in the library was to find the book you mentioned. I agree entirely with your statement, my love. Shall we leave that decision until after the ceremony?'

Her smile made her even more lovely. 'Thank you for being so understanding. I should also like to thank you for bringing me to my apartment, but could I request that in future you do not sling me over your shoulder in such an undignified manner?'

'I'll agree to your request if you

promise not to drop things on my head in future.'

'That's an easy one to make. Did you have your supper?' From the plaintive note in her voice he suspected she might be hungry.

'I did, but I shall go and fetch you something similar. I had no coffee so I'll bring that as well.'

She picked up the bell and rang it. A maid appeared at the bedchamber door. 'Kindly bring some coffee plus whatever's available in the kitchen.' The girl curtsied and vanished. 'I should have asked for a tray to be sent up at dinner time but had no appetite then. Now I find myself quite ravenous.'

He strolled across and picked up the book she'd discarded. 'Some Gothic nonsense I perceive — small wonder those monks found you receptive.'

'I've always been interested in the spirit world. I believe it's because I hoped my parents would come and speak to me directly.'

'I was told I would meet mine again

in heaven which was some comfort at the time.' He changed the subject, talking about his parents was not something he enjoyed. 'Do you have an ensemble in mind for our wedding?'

'I'm so glad you asked. Grandmother is, as no doubt you have noticed, very short-sighted so there's no point in asking her opinion. I have chosen three that might be possible and would be so pleased if you could make the final selection for me.' She smiled ruefully. 'Although, I rather think it matters little what I have on as I'll be obliged to wear my cloak so it will not be seen.'

'It will be on view when we return here, won't it?' He nodded towards the bedchamber. 'Are they in your closet or on display?'

'The latter. I'll not tell you which one I prefer and just hope you make the same choice.'

He pushed open the door and immediately saw the gowns. He didn't need to examine them — he knew at once which one would be perfect. It was a dark green velvet with emerald decorations around the neck and hem. It was the perfect match for her beautiful eyes. He ignored the other two and returned to her sitting room.

'The green — no question about it.'

'It's the one I like best too. I hope you have something equally impressive to wear on our wedding day.'

'I have a topcoat almost the same hue as your gown and a green silk waistcoat the colour of your eyes. I think we'll be a handsome couple.'

'More importantly, Garrick, I truly think we shall be a happy couple, which is far more important in my opinion.'

8

Eloise watched the man she was about to marry fold his long length onto the chair opposite. The more time they spent together the happier she was about this arranged marriage. There could not be another gentleman in the world who would not only be happy to marry someone with her infirmity, but also to accept the fact that they were plagued by ghosts.

'I doubt that you will have a scar when the stitches are removed. Even if you do it won't show as your hair falls across the injury.'

'They will be removed before the ceremony. I want to look my best for you.'

She wasn't sure at first if he was jesting or serious but then the expression in his eyes told her he meant every word. Was he beginning to have feelings for her as she was for him?

The rattle of crockery interrupted their conversation. Polly came herself this time and pushed open the sitting room door and held it whilst two footmen staggered in with laden trays. Her maid set out the table and then curtsied and left them alone.

'Remain where you are, sweetheart, I know what to do.' He grinned over his shoulder as he picked up a plate. 'This is an excellent spread and more than enough for both of us.'

'I should think so — I might be hungry but I doubt even I can devour more than a fraction of what has been fetched.'

Whilst he was dishing up, she swung her legs to the floor and waited eagerly to see what he'd given her. She had expected him to give her far too much but what he handed her was perfect. She waited for him to return to his place with his own food before picking up her cutlery.

Despite her claim that there was too

much on the table, by the time they had had several helpings there wasn't much left. She was sipping her third cup of coffee when something rattled the window. Her heart leapt, her hand jerked and the contents of the cup flew into the air to land on the priceless rug.

He was beside her in a second. 'There's nothing to be afraid of, my love, they cannot reach us here. It was merely a gust of wind.'

'I know it was. I was never bothered by them before because I knew they wouldn't hurt me. I couldn't bear it if anything were to happen to you because you came here for me.'

He removed the empty cup from her fingers and then sat beside her. 'I came here for myself originally, and for my grandfather, but everything changed when you galloped past me. I wish to marry you because I love you.'

For a moment she couldn't comprehend what he'd said. Then, she flung her arms around his neck. 'I love you too.' He kissed her; a brief, hard press of his lips, but it was enough to seal their new accord.

When she'd recovered her composure, she smiled shyly. 'I cannot understand how our feelings have been so quickly engaged. I know nothing of such matters, as you might imagine.'

He took her hand and raised it to his lips. Her stomach clenched in anticipation. That familiar rush of heat engulfed her. His eyes were dark. How could someone as flawed as she have such an effect on him?

'Darling girl, I cannot wait to show you how much I love you.'

He kissed each knuckle in turn and the touch of his lips made her want to throw herself back into his arms but discovering the pleasures of the marital state must wait until they were wed.

'I don't want to leave you alone if you're worried about unwanted visitors during the night.'

She giggled quite inappropriately. 'The only unwanted visitor I'm worried about is yourself, my love. I think it best if you go away now before we do something we shouldn't.'

'Listen — is that rain I can hear on the window panes?' Without being asked, he went to the window, parted the curtains, and pulled the shutters open just enough to see the glass. 'Yes, the thaw has begun. I'm not sure if that's a good thing or not.'

She recalled what they'd discussed before about it being better there weren't guests staying with them over Christmas. 'This will be my grandfather's final Christmas and I want it to be special. Having people staying here, listening to them enjoying themselves, is exactly what we all need at the moment.'

He didn't return to his position beside her but headed for the door. 'I believe you told me the monks have been haunting the Priory for centuries. There must be a mention of them in a journal or notebook — are there such things anywhere? Also, why has no one tried to exorcise them? I think it might be worth trying, as matters could not be worse than they are at present.'

'The curate is coming tomorrow to discuss the wedding. We must ask him to perform an exorcism, but I think he might well cavil at the prospect. It means going inside the rooms I used to inhabit. I'm not sure that would be safe for anyone now.'

'Journals? What about them? They might well hold valuable clues as to the reason these ghosts have remained here and not passed over. They were men of God and surely they must wish to worship at his feet and not lurk about here causing havoc?'

'Whilst the curate is performing the ceremony, that is, if he agrees to do so, I shall go to the library and seek out the books you mention. I'm certain there's a shelf full of such things somewhere.'

'On that note I'll take my leave. Good night, sweetheart, I'm counting the hours until I can remain here with you.'

He was gone before she could gather

her wits and reply. No sooner had the door closed than Polly bustled in and piled the debris onto the trays.

'My Tom says the snow will be quite gone in a day or two but the roads will be nigh on impassable for at least another week unless it freezes.'

'That's true. The snow will leave the roads and lanes knee-deep in mud. Even if it does freeze, I doubt that even a rider would get through without his horse breaking a leg. I cannot decide if I'm happy or disappointed that we're unlikely to get any visitors.'

'Don't you fret, my lamb, it'll be a wonderful Christmas with or without guests. I can't tell you how happy the staff are that you're getting wed and to such a handsome gentleman.'

'Polly, can I tell you a secret?'

'La, Miss Eloise, it's no secret that you and he are head over heels in love. The good Lord sent him to us and you're made for each other. He'll look after you and be a good husband and father to any little ones you have.'

An hour later she was under the comforter but too excited to sleep. It was as if an unseen hand was spinning her world around, leaving her no time to catch her breath or quite grasp what was happening as everything moved on so quickly.

The catalyst had been the arrival of Garrick. People said that God moved in mysterious ways and after the past week she would have to agree. It was as if she was being hurried towards something cataclysmic and she wasn't sure if what was going to happen would be joyful or the opposite.

*   *   *

Garrick sprung out of bed with more enthusiasm than he could ever remember. Being in love was not something he'd ever expected to experience himself but now he was in the throes of this emotion, he was enjoying every minute. He prayed that this feeling was permanent, that it wouldn't evaporate when reality took over. Even if things became more settled between them, he would never change his mind. Whatever life had in store for them, one thing he was quite certain of was that his love for Eloise was deep and abiding and nothing could come between them — not even ghosts.

The rain was still hammering down and the snow had all but gone. He'd never known such changeable weather and was beginning to suspect the extraordinary events at the Priory might well be linked to what was happening outside.

He smiled at his foolishness. But then a chill slithered down his spine as if cold fingers had touched him. Ghosts were unbelievable — so was it so far-fetched to think that they could control the elements as well as their surroundings?

As they'd been trapped here he'd no notion if the inclement weather had been experienced elsewhere or just in their immediate vicinity. Devil take it! If his outlandish theory was correct then they could expect the house guests to turn up next week as planned as they wouldn't be aware the lanes around the Priory were impassable.

He banged on her door but didn't wait to be invited inside. She appeared from her bedchamber in a voluminous nightgown. 'What are you doing here so early? As you can see I've yet to get up and my maid's only just gone down to fetch my hot water.'

His heart lurched at the way she was obliged to clutch onto the door frame in order to keep her balance. 'My darling, I must speak to you immediately. Are you going to remain in the doorway or will you come and join me in here?'

Her delightful laughter filled the room. 'Go away, Garrick, I've absolutely no intention of holding a conversation with you in my nightgown.'

'I can assure you that your innocence is in no danger, my love, when dressed in that hideous garment.' His smile was wicked as he moved closer. 'However, if you will allow me to remove it . . . '

He expected her to blush and retreat but she did the opposite. She reached out and moved into his embrace. 'I should like nothing better than to discover the delights of making love with you. I'm not certain that Polly will appreciate the spectacle but . . . '

He lifted her from her feet and kissed her until she was breathless. Then he shouldered his way into her bedchamber and placed her, none too gently, on her bed. 'You, my dear, are a baggage. I'll come back in half an hour. I suggest that you're dressed by then or I vow I'll take you at your word.'

He was laughing out loud as he bounded down the stairs. He'd already sent his valet to the stables with the letters that had yet to be posted. A groom was to take them to the nearest inn at which the mail coach stopped.

If the lowering clouds and icy rain was as local as he suspected then he would know shortly. What he would do with that knowledge he'd no idea, but he'd share it with his beloved at the earliest possible opportunity.

He snapped his fingers and a vigilant footman appeared at his side. 'Send word to the kitchen that no breakfast is to be served downstairs today. Have trays sent up to Miss Eloise's sitting room for us both.'

He enjoyed carrying her about the place but there was no need for her to be downstairs until midday when Lady Granville would be in the drawing room. Eloise should by rights be referred to as Miss Granville as she was not only the eldest daughter of the house, but the only one. In ten days' time she would be Lady Forsyth and he could hardly contain his impatience.

Then he recalled her saying the cleric would be coming later today — he could have waited and asked him if the village was also cut off by the weather. It was no more than half a mile from the Priory, easy enough to walk even in these conditions, so he could see no difficulty with the man coming for his meeting.

Despite the miserable weather conditions, he was in the best of spirits. He was so happy he thought he might pen a sonnet or two praising the beauty of her eyes. He was still smiling at his nonsense when he strolled into her sitting room no more than ten minutes since he had vacated it.

The bedroom door was firmly shut as if she'd anticipated his early return. He moved the circular table from its position by the window and carried it to the centre of the room, then he arranged two chairs on opposite sides. Next, he collected the various items displayed on top of the bureau and put them on the mantelshelf.

Satisfied that when the breakfast arrived there would be room to put the dishes out as if they were downstairs, he wandered across to look at the books on her well-stocked bookshelf. There were half a dozen romances, which he'd expected to see, but also several titles of a more serious nature, which surprised him.

The door behind him opened and he turned to greet her. 'Good morning again, my love. Permit me to say I much prefer the ensemble you have on now.'

'Green is my favourite colour, no doubt you've noticed that.' She raised a hand when he moved to help her. 'No, much as I like being supported by you, I'm quite capable of moving about the place myself, albeit rather slowly and awkwardly.'

Something belatedly occurred to him. 'Surely you would progress more smoothly if you used a cane?'

'I'm sure you're correct but using one would make me feel not only crippled but like an old woman.'

'Absolute nonsense! I'm going to find one immediately and insist that you use it in future.'

'You don't have far to look, there are a selection at the back of my closet. Feel free to bring one you think will suit. I cannot promise that I'll use it.' She moved to one side to let him pass but remained in the doorway watching him examine the canes.

He selected one with silver filigree and jade insets. Perfect, as it would complement any outfit rather than detract from it.

'Here you are. Will you try it for me?' He brushed her cheek with his hand as he passed and she turned her face to lean it against him for a second.

Three footmen arrived at the sitting room door with their breakfast and they needed no telling to place them on the sideboard. Then a fourth deftly flipped a white tablecloth over the table and put out the silver cutlery, condiments and cups. The coffee jug was given central position. The four of them bowed and left them to it which was exactly as it should be.

He deliberately kept his back to her so she could practice walking without being observed.

'You may turn around now, Garrick, I've mastered my cane.'

'Show me. Am I right? Is it easier

with or without it?'

Her smile was blinding as she moved more quickly and with more elegance than she had before. 'I can be stubborn, but on this occasion I'm forced to admit I've made my life more difficult by refusing to use one of these.'

He pulled out a chair and she sat with more grace than she'd ever been able to display before. 'If you pour the coffee, I'll bring the food.'

* * *

Breakfast had never tasted so delicious and Eloise enjoyed every mouthful. There was obviously something he wished to tell her and it must be important if he was leaving it until they were replete. Eventually she dropped her cutlery, wiped her mouth on the napkin and was ready to hear whatever it was he had to tell her. When he had done she was amazed.

'Do you really think the phenomena taking place here is also affecting the weather? Two weeks ago I'd have thought you fit for Bedlam, but now I believe you might be right.'

'If I am, then it presents all sorts of other dilemmas. Heavy snow falling only on this estate and nowhere else, and then torrential rain — this cannot fail to have been noted by your neighbours.'

'I see what you're suggesting. Such extraordinary events might well alarm them and make them wish to keep away. On the other hand, those that live further afield and who were intending to stay for the festive season as well as our marriage will already be making their way here completely unaware that anything unusual has occurred.'

'Exactly so. They will have no difficulty travelling until they reach this vicinity. Then, I fear, they will be unable to progress. I've sent a groom with some letters and he will be able to confirm or deny our supposition.'

'I refuse to dwell on such things when I am so happy. I think that we would not have fallen in love so quickly without the intervention of these ghosts, so for that I shall be thankful.'

His smile made her toes curl. 'I too will be forever grateful that I came here despite the unusual circumstances surrounding your home. We have lingered here too long already; I'm hoping that the groom will have returned from his errand by now as he left at first light.'

He was behind her in an instant and lifted her and the chair away from the table. She had dropped her pretty cane and he stooped to collect it. 'There, I'll not assist you. From now on I'm certain you will be able to move about more comfortably and will no longer require my help.'

Standing up presented her with no difficulty and she was able to join him by the door without being obliged to clutch onto something to keep herself upright. Pride was indeed a dangerous thing and hers had kept her from accepting that she needed help to walk.

'I know you said you would carry me

down the stairs but I should like to attempt them on my own. If I struggle you have my permission to step in.'

When they reached the staircase he moved slightly ahead of her and was ready to catch her in case she missed her footing. It took longer to descend than it would have done if she were not lame but at no time did she feel herself in danger of falling.

His arm encircled her waist as she took the last step and arrived safely in the hall. 'Well done, darling girl. I think with a little more practice you will be able to ascend and descend stairs with no difficulty.'

'I still intend to have that operation. I wish to be able to run after my children, play with them in the garden and even with my cane I shall not be able to do so. Neither will I be able to carry them myself as to do so requires both arms.'

He hugged her tight. 'I've already told you I'll support whatever decision you make.' He drew her to one side where they could not be overheard by the footman who stood on guard in the hall to open doors and run errands when required.

'If you have made your decision then I shall not share your bed until it's done . . . '

'Fiddlesticks to that! There's no urgency for the procedure to be performed — it can wait, if necessary, until after our first child is born.'

9

This was a most unsuitable conversation to be holding even though it was with her future husband. Eloise cared not about such niceties. The thought of what they had to do in order to produce this first infant made her tingle all over and from the darkness in his eyes she was certain he was equally eager to begin their married life.

'Dear girl, do you both intend to dawdle out there indefinitely or are you coming in to sit with us?'

'Grandpapa, if I'd known you were down so early of course we would have been here.' Using her new stick, she was able to reach his side in record time. 'You look so much better than you did a few days ago. In fact, your colour is now a healthy pink and no longer yellow.'

'If I did not know that my situation is

terminal I would think I was recovering. As soon as the rain abates I shall send for the physician and get him to examine me.'

Her grandmother was smiling and this was a rare occurrence lately. 'Sit down both of you, there are things we need to discuss.'

Garrick bowed politely but did not take a seat. 'Forgive me, but I have business to attend to. It won't take long and then I'll join you.'

He strode off and the room seemed strangely flat without him in it. She quickly explained his theory and instead of laughing they exchanged a glance and nodded.

'This was what we wished to speak to you about, my dear. I've had the outside-men clearing the worst of the mud from the lanes and the head gardener came to see me half an hour ago. No snow has fallen anywhere but here — the rain is also limited to this estate.'

They agreed that it made sense to ask

the curate to try and drive the brothers from the Priory. 'He should be here shortly to discuss our wedding service — but the exorcism must come first.'

'Exactly what happens in this ceremony?' Grandmama asked.

'I've no idea, but I'll go and search the library here. It's possible there's something hidden away on one of the shelves, especially as these ghosts have been in residence for centuries. I wonder if this house was built here because of them?'

'It's certainly of more recent construction than the Priory, my dear, but as far as I know it was just for lay visitors.'

'I'll be back in time to speak to the curate, Grandpapa. It's possible, of course, that he won't wish to do it, in which case we'll have to do it ourselves.'

The library visit proved unsuccessful and she had just returned the last book to the shelf when Garrick arrived. One look at his face was enough to tell her his suspicions had been confirmed.

'What is the weather like away from the estate?'

'Bright winter sunshine, clear skies and just a heavy frost at night. The groom handed in his notice on his return and has already left. I fear he won't be the only one to depart today. I came to fetch you as the curate is here.'

'Is the rain showing any sign of abating? I must ensure the poor man has dry clothes before he is obliged to hear our request.'

'The housekeeper has already taken care of that. He's with your grandparents and seems unperturbed by the strange goings-on here.'

He, naturally, slowed his pace to suit her, but using her cane meant she could walk quite briskly and without lurching from side to side as she had before.

'Does our visitor know what we require of him today?'

'Not as yet. Sir Thomas has asked me to explain — but I'm quite happy to let you take the lead as you know more about these ghosts than I do.'

From the sound of the chatter drifting from the drawing room, none of the occupants were in any way upset about the unusual situation they found themselves in. This was a good sign.

The cleric jumped to his feet and bowed to both of them as they walked in. She nodded as did Garrick and they took their places opposite the other three.

The young man listened attentively to both her and Garrick's explanation. 'Murdered you say? I believe the spirits cannot pass over because of the way they died. I think, my lord, Miss Granville, together we can assist them to leave.

'I've never conducted an exorcism but have read widely on the subject. The important thing is that we all go properly equipped. We need to carry a cross and to recite the Lord's Prayer continuously whilst sprinkling holy water about the place.'

'And then what?' Garrick said.

'Then, my lord, I shall recite the

necessary words and shall entreat them to depart. It is crucial that one believes in what one speaks, and that one remains calm and pushes one's fear aside.'

Eloise came to a decision and it was one that she thought would not be appreciated by her beloved. 'As we explained, sir, they only became violent when they knew I was to marry. I believe it would be better if his lordship remained here as his presence will antagonise them.'

Unexpectedly he agreed. 'I'll come with you but remain outside, or in the stables if the rain persists.'

'I've ordered a closed carriage to transport you — the weather is too inclement for walking half a mile.'

'Thank you, Grandpapa, I was going to do so myself. That means, my lord, that you can remain dry and yet still be close.'

The carriage was outside by the time she returned suitably dressed in her outdoor garments. Garrick had on his caped riding coat and the clergyman had borrowed a cloak. The footmen escorted them to the vehicle holding umbrellas above their heads.

No one spoke on the short journey but her hand was in his and the contact was enough to give her the courage to descend when they rocked to a halt.

'How long is this likely to take?'

'Hopefully no more than half an hour, my lord.'

'In which case I'll not remain here, as the horses need to be under cover.'

He came with them to the front door but remained a yard away. 'If you're not out in the allotted time I shall come in to find you.' He tapped his waistcoat pocket, indicating he had his watch with him.

'I'll go first, sir, they know me and will cause no problems.' She said this with bravado and prayed she was correct. 'Do you have holy water about your person?'

The curate shook his head. 'I thought to obtain some in your chapel. The water used for the font has been blessed and there's a jug kept in a cupboard to be used in the event of a family christening.'

'Good heavens! Will it still be effective, as it must be years old?'

'Miss Granville, it's holy water, not a common liquid.'

He sounded quite offended at her query and she was glad he was so sure of this one thing as nothing about this enterprise seemed at all certain. The ghosts had occupied the Priory since the dissolution of the monasteries by Henry VIII and there must have been others who had tried to dislodge them — so why were they still there?

It had never occurred to her to ask them such a question but she would do so today before they started on the ritual.

'I shall obtain the necessary holy water, Miss Granville, whilst you locate these beings.'

In order to reach the chapel there was no necessity to enter the main house so he would be in no danger — as a man of the cloth she hoped he would not be in danger anywhere.

In their rush to leave, the house had not been locked. Why should anyone wish to go in there when it was occupied by spirits? On stepping into the hall, she was immediately aware the brothers were waiting for her. At first, they were not visible but when she moved into the centre of the vast space they began to take shape.

'I'm glad that you are all here, as there is something I wish to ask you.'

'Where have you been? Why have you abandoned us?'

'I left because you threatened to kill the man I love. Tell me, why you have not gone to join the Almighty in heaven? You were men of God and will surely be eagerly received by the angels.'

The insubstantial forms swirled around her, their ghostly fingers brushing her cheeks. Had she misjudged the situation? Or was she no longer exempted from their anger?

'We wish to go but something is preventing us from leaving.'

'Then you'll not object when the curate and I do our best to help you pass over?'

'Many have tried, but none were successful.' The speaker was Brother James. If he was eager to depart from the Priory then she was certain the other three would also wish to go.

'Have you been able to communicate directly with anyone living here before me?'

The shapes shimmered and Brother Francis, the monk who had acted as doorman for her, took shape before her. 'No, you are the first and only living being who can speak to us. That is why we don't wish you to leave.'

'I understand your reasons. I think now is the perfect time for you to cross over to the other side. I believe that I am unique and together we can achieve this if you will cooperate.'

'If your betrothed were here, it would make you stronger and the possibility of us leaving more likely.'

The conversation was interrupted

when the cleric stepped in. Instantly the spirits retreated as if afraid of him.

'We need to go to the library immediately. I wish to check something. There's a history of the Priory which I've never read and I think there will be something about how the monks were murdered.'

She led the way through the icy passages, glad she had put on her warmest garments. Even with her gloves on, her fingers were turning numb. He hurried along beside her.

'What is it you wish to know, Miss Granville?'

'I cannot think why this did not occur to me before now. There must have been dozens of monks residing here — why would only these four have remained behind?'

'Possibly the others left the premises peacefully and died elsewhere. These four must have refused to leave and thus been killed by the King's men.'

The book she wanted had been written by her great-grandfather, who she had been told was a bad-tempered and stern man. For this reason, she'd never bothered to read his account.

'See, I was right. The monks left peaceably — none were killed — yet there are four here who claim to have been murdered.' The ink had faded over time and the spidery writing was hard to decipher. She flicked back and her knees almost folded beneath her when she saw the reason these ghosts were still here.

The cleric read over her shoulder and his shocked gasp echoed around the icy room. 'These were evil men, not monks at all. They were incarcerated in the dungeons for heinous crimes against the villagers. All four of them died here. It is small wonder that they refuse to leave as they would be going to the other place and not to join the Almighty.'

'I fear it's going to be nigh on impossible to make them depart, but we'll do our best. I wish I'd read this before I became entangled with them.'

'They would have sought you out

eventually, even if you hadn't moved into those rooms.'

It had taken them a considerable time to locate the book and read the necessary passages. A sick dread engulfed her when she heard Garrick calling her name in the passageway outside.

She snatched up her cane and hurried to the door. They arrived simultaneously. He took one look at her face and understood at once something was wrong.

'Tell me, what has changed so drastically?'

Whilst she explained, the curate sprinkled holy water about them and no sooner had the circle been completed than her fear evaporated. They were safe from harm — at least for the moment.

'I was almost impaled on a spear as I crossed the hall. I clutched onto the crucifix and recited the Lord's Prayer as loudly as I could and I believe only that kept me safe.'

'I have the words we need to say to try and force these entities to go. *Ecce crusis signum; fugiant phantasmata cuncta.* The Latin translated means this: *behold the emblem of the cross; let all spectres flee.'*

They repeated it several times with him until they knew it off by heart. She took out the chain she wore around her neck and held the cross tightly in one hand. Garrick followed suit. The cleric held his aloft in one hand whilst having the holy water ready to sprinkle in the other.

Her heart was pounding. If anything happened to him she would never forgive herself. This was a foolhardy expedition and she regretted agreeing to do it.

'I'll not let anything harm you, my love, together we shall prevail.' As soon as his arm was around her waist not only was she steadier on her feet but her fear began to recede and her courage returned.

* * *

The question was not whether he could protect her, but if the holy water, crosses and chanting would be sufficient to keep the ghosts from murdering him. It had been a close thing just now when he'd hurtled through the Priory looking for Eloise.

'I can feel them in the room. Can you see them, sweetheart?'

'No, I think the holy water has created a barrier. I can sense them too. Shall we begin?'

There was no need to go in search of the apparitions as they were surrounding them. They moved forward as one with the curate at the front and they alternated the chant in Latin with the prayer. The malevolence, the evil emanating from these spectres, washed over them.

As had happened in the gatehouse, he began to feel the breath being drawn from his chest by icy fingers. He held tighter to the crucifix, raised his voice and he yelled the Latin words. She copied him, as did the curate. Breathing was becoming more difficult. He redoubled his efforts and was then lifted bodily from the floor and thrown across the passageway. The world turned black and there was a fearsome screaming and then he was free.

Eloise had been torn from his hold. He'd cracked his head on the wall, but the damage was to the back of his crown, not his forehead, this time. He heaved himself to his feet, dreading what he might see.

She was spreadeagled on the flag-stones, arms outstretched, her face paper-white but she was still breathing. He gathered her in his arms and held her close. The young curate was stagger-ing to his feet. The flagon of holy water smashed on the stones. The pool of water glowed with a golden light for a moment and he thought he had imag-ined it.

'They've gone, my lord, we forced them to leave. They are where they deserve to be and face eternal damna-tion. The Priory's no longer haunted.'

He scarcely heard these words, so concerned was he about her. Then she stirred and he could breathe again. 'Darling girl, we succeeded. We've driven them away and for the first time in centuries this house is safe to live in.'

Slowly, the colour returned to her cheeks. 'It's as if a weight has been lifted from my shoulders. I cannot believe we managed it.' He helped her to regain her feet and smiled at the young man whose knowledge had saved them all.

'We have you to thank, we could not have done this without your assistance. Listen, the rain has stopped and I do believe the sun is shining.'

'It's damn cold in here, I suggest we continue this conversation when we're safely back. I sincerely hope Sir Thomas will not wish to return here — it's far more comfortable where we are.'

'Grandmama and I will persuade him to remain where he is. However, we can now be married in the chapel rather than the village church.'

They emerged into the courtyard to find it full of terrified grooms and outside-men. His valet was the only one capable of speaking.

'We've never seen the like, my lord. Terrible screaming, flashing lights and then what seemed like an explosion knocked us from our feet. Then, miraculously, the clouds vanished and the sun came out. What in God's name happened in there?'

'The exorcism was successful.' Garrick raised his voice so the men could hear him clearly. 'The ghosts have gone; St Cuthbert's Priory is no longer haunted. From now on it will be perfectly safe to reside here.'

His coachman appeared from the carriage house driving his own vehicle. His valet let down the steps and Garrick lifted Eloise inside. He turned to beckon the cleric to enter next but the young man shook his head.

He moved closer and spoke softly. 'No, my lord, I have work to do here if you don't wish to lose every man who witnessed what happened.'

'Good man, do what you can to

rectify the situation.'

He jumped inside and the carriage rocked a second time as his valet clambered onto the back step. He could hardly believe they'd been successful in their venture.

'I don't think this would have worked if you'd not been there, Garrick. I think they were concentrating so hard on trying to kill you that they were unable to protect themselves from the words and the holy water. To think I've been communicating with murderers these past four years.'

'And from now on you shall be with me. I had few expectations when I set out and yet here I am neck over crop in love with you and we have just successfully dispatched your ghosts.'

'Life from now on is going to seem decidedly dull . . . '

Despite the fact that the carriage was just rolling to a halt and at any moment the door would be opened, he pulled her onto his lap. 'I can assure you, darling girl, your life is going to be anything but dull.' To prove his point he covered her mouth with his and it was a considerable time later that they eventually emerged from the carriage.

10

The next few days flew past and, apart from a dozen polite notes regretting the writers were no longer able to attend the celebrations, everything was going smoothly. Eloise had convinced her grandparents to remain where they were as the house was more convenient and far warmer than the vast, ancient Priory.

'All the guests that we've invited to stay over the festive period are still coming, it is only those who live locally that have refused, and who can blame them?' Her grandmother was not unduly bothered so neither would she be.

'As you're not intending to live here for much longer I hardly think it matters if your neighbours no longer wish to associate with you. I am quite certain that in a few weeks everyone

180

will have forgotten and be eager to renew contact with your grandfather and me.'

'It will be a sad crush,' Grandmama said, 'when everyone is here, but Bates assured me we can accommodate everyone including their personal staff.'

'The physician is astonished at the change in Grandpapa's health. I'm beginning to suspect it was living in such close proximity to those evil spirits that was making him so unwell. If he continues to improve at this rate then there will be no necessity for you to come with us to Penston or for us to remain here after Twelfth Night.'

'For the first time in months he has gone out to inspect his lands. He wished to reassure his tenants and villagers that, despite the extraordinary occurrences here, they had nothing further to fear. It's fortuitous that we were overstaffed as so many of them have departed.'

'As you say, Grandmama, those who have remained are more than adequate for our needs. I cannot tell you how glad I am that we will only be moving fifty miles away. When the weather improves I'm hoping you will both make a prolonged stay at our new home. The journey will no longer be a barrier.'

'This is a Christmas like no other I can remember. Not only are you to marry the gentleman you have fallen in love with, and my dearest Thomas has made a miraculous recovery — but also the unwanted occupants of the Priory have gone for good.'

'As I haven't seen Garrick this morning I must assume he has gone out with Grandpapa. I'm eager to have the festive decorations on display. Do I have your permission to ask the footmen to begin the task of putting up the garlands, kissing-boughs, wreaths and other items? I know it's customary to wait until the day before Christmas Eve but I think we should celebrate early.'

'I am before you, my dear, the matter

is already in hand. I think it better the staff that have remained in our employ are fully occupied and have no time to dwell on why the others handed in their notice. You will be married in less than a week and the first of the house guests will be arriving the day after tomorrow. The house must be ready by then.'

Garrick returned to find the place in disarray and was obliged to pick his way through piles of winter greenery in order to reach the drawing room. She had watched him with amusement from her position on the daybed. She had selected her place as it was the only one that gave her an unrestricted view of the hall.

'How long is this nonsense going to take, Eloise?'

'Everywhere apart from here will be done today. They will decorate the drawing room first thing tomorrow morning.' He dropped down beside her and immediately lifted her onto his lap. 'You must not make a habit of this, my love, from tomorrow there will be strangers here.'

'Are you objecting to my actions, sweetheart?'

She tilted her face and made it perfectly clear she was as eager as he to exchange kisses. A delightful and stimulating time later they reluctantly parted. She wriggled off his lap to sit a sensible distance from him.

'Was the ride successful? It would seem that you will not be in charge of this estate after all. What will you do about the man you have already invited to take it over?'

'Sir Thomas and I have discussed this. My man will come as planned and live in the Priory. Your grandfather has decided to retire and is happy to hand over the reins to me; I shall then hand the estate on to my estate manager. In future, your grandparents will live here in a degree more comfort than they ever had at the other place.'

'This will be the last family dinner we share before the house is invaded. I warn you, my love, they are not friends of mine but of my grandparents. When

I looked at the guest list I swore there was no one remotely close to us in age.'

He chuckled. 'It was the same when we entertained at Penston. There are younger families in the neighbourhood and we will send out cards and invite them to an informal supper party as soon as we're settled.'

'Would you prefer to wait until I'm no longer lame?'

'God's teeth! How many times do I have to tell you that to me you're perfect and I don't give a damn what anyone else thinks. However, if you would rather postpone our socialising until your leg has been reset and you are back on your feet, then so be it. The decision is yours.'

'I wish I could speak to the surgeon who will be doing the operation and find out exactly how long I will be recuperating. It's difficult to make plans without having that information.'

'I've sent for Doctor Mathews so he may examine you immediately. He might well arrive tomorrow along with the guests. He will not expect to stay here — my valet has booked accommodation for him at The Red Lion.'

'You are the kindest of gentlemen and I am so lucky to be marrying you. I know I'm inexperienced in the ways of the world, but I'm intelligent and will soon adapt to my new life. I promise that I'll not let you down.'

His eyes blazed and he took her hands in his. 'It is I that am the lucky one, darling girl, I honestly believe that we were destined to be together.'

The tall-case clock in the far corner struck the hour. 'We must go and change for dinner. I have no wish to be tardy tonight. I warn you that I shall be wearing an evening gown so I expect you to make the same effort with your apparel.'

He held out his hand and pulled her easily to her feet and then placed her cane in her hand. 'Might I enquire, sweetheart, what colour your gown will be?'

'It is duck-egg blue, an unusual

shade, but when the seamstress came from London to attend me she assured me it's all the rage there.'

He kept his arm around her waist even though she was quite capable of walking safely without his support. She loved leaning against him, feeling his strength, his warmth, hard against her softness.

*   *   *

Garrick burst into his dressing room to accost his valet. 'Do I have a waistcoat in duck-egg blue or something similar?'

'Eau de Nil? I believe you do, my lord. It's not a colour you approved of so has never been worn.'

'Excellent. The house will be invaded tomorrow, I wish you to help out in any way you can. If a gentleman has not brought his own manservant, you will offer your services.'

'I shall be happy to do so, my lord. I have already told the housekeeper I am prepared to share my accommodation. The room I have been allocated has two beds so it would be mean-spirited of me to remain in there alone.'

Garrick lingered in his sitting room flicking through a journal, waiting to hear Sir Thomas and his wife go past so he could go in to Eloise. He left it too late as she was in the passageway when he stepped out.

'Good evening, my love. Might I say that look you particularly lovely? That ensemble is a triumph.'

Her gurgle of laughter made him smile. 'That's doing it a bit too brown, but the compliment is much appreciated. My word, your waistcoat is a perfect match to my gown.'

He put his arm around her waist as always and dropped a light kiss on the top of her elaborately coiffured hair. 'I aim to please. Although I'm forced to admit I heartily dislike this colour.'

She glanced up at him with a mischievous smile. 'Then your admiration of my gown is false. You're a charlatan, my lord, and I fear I've made the most dreadful error in agreeing to become your wife.'

He lifted her from her feet and was about to show her just how wrong she was when she wriggled free. 'Look at that, Garrick. Have you ever seen anything so beautiful?'

She was staring wide-eyed at the finished decorations in the hall below. He had not thought he would like such nonsense but she was right. It did look stunning. 'I don't believe I have — apart from yourself, of course. I never imagined that strewing the place with garlands of greenery, candles and ribbons could make so much difference.'

'Quickly, we must go down so I can examine it all before we dine.' She breathed in and exhaled with a sigh. 'I can smell the yule log burning and I believe applewood has also been put in with it. I fear you will be most displeased with what I have decided.'

'The answer is a categorical no, so do not even suggest it.'

Instead of being put out by his answer she laughed out loud. 'We both know that if I wish to decorate Penston, I shall get my own way. You can deny me nothing.'

Ignoring the smiling footman, he spun her so she was pressed hard against him and then stopped her silliness with his lips. She melted into him and returned his kiss with equal enthusiasm. Eventually he raised his head.

'It's fortunate, sweetheart, that we are standing beneath the kissing-bough or we should be in disgrace.'

'With whom? My grandparents are not stuffy in the slightest and there is no one else to disapprove. If we wish to embrace then we shall do so.'

He led her through the hall and was obliged to stop frequently in order for her to examine and exclaim over each frill and furbelow. Sir Thomas and his wife were waiting patiently to go through to the dining room.

'Grandmama, Grandpapa, doesn't the house look splendid in its festive finery? I apologise if I kept you waiting but I had to look at everything.'

'I must say I'm delighted with the change the decorations have made to the place, Eloise; I'm sure our guests will be equally impressed. Now, child, hurry up as dinner will be spoiled if we do not go through.' The spectacular orange ostrich feathers in Lady Granville's turban bounced up and down as she spoke.

Sir Thomas took his wife's arm and all four of them progressed to the central door that led directly into the dining room. This too had been decorated. However, this had not been done with garlands but with elegant arrangements of greenery.

The meal was sumptuous; three courses each with several removes. Wine and champagne flowed. Garrick had consumed more than enough himself and suspected Eloise was in her cups. He feared she might fall if she did not have control of her limbs.

'Forgive us, Sir Thomas, Lady Granville, if we do not join you in the drawing room. Eloise has imbibed rather too much alcohol and I shall carry her to her bedchamber.'

There was no argument on this score even from his love who appeared to have nodded off. He scooped her up and carried his precious burden through the house to deposit her gently on her bed where her dresser was waiting to do her duty.

It was far too early to retire and for some reason he did not wish to return to the drawing room. He spent some time admiring the lavish arrangements and then was about to retreat to the library where he could be certain he would be undisturbed when there was a thunderous knocking on the door.

There were no guests expected to arrive tonight. He remained in the hall, curious to see who it could be. A footman opened the door and if his intention was to block the entrance of whoever it was, he failed miserably.

'I have had a wretched journey; I should have been here hours ago. I am Lady Sarah Dunstable, a personal friend of Lord Forsyth. I have come to see him married.'

For a second Garrick was unable to function. How the devil had she discovered his whereabouts so quickly? Her arrival could only spell disaster. He regained the ability to think coherently, schooled his features to hide his dismay, and moved smoothly into the centre of the hall.

'My lady, you did not receive an invitation to visit here. You are *de trop*.' He pointed to the still open front door. 'I shall escort you back to your carriage. You will find accommodation at The Red Lion, no more than two miles from here.'

He remained firmly in front of her and was aware that the footmen were now standing at either shoulder. He sent up a fervent prayer to the Almighty that whatever happened next, Eloise would not hear of it. At any moment he expected Lady Granville to demand to be introduced.

Sarah remained where she was, her expression arctic. 'Garrick, I am prepared to make the most appalling scene, one that your reputation will not recover from, if you try and eject me from this house.'

For a second he considered calling her bluff but realised he had no option but to allow her in. By doing so he possibly risked losing Eloise, but if he did not, and she did create a fuss, then he was certain Eloise would break off the betrothal.

'Very well, you may stay here tonight. But tomorrow you will leave even if I have to remove you bodily myself. I can't imagine what you hoped to achieve by coming here.'

Her eyes were like flint, her lips thinned as she answered. 'Can you not? I find that I am carrying your child. Do you wish your firstborn to be a bastard?'

She had spoken just loud enough to be overheard by the watching servants. She saw the murder in his eyes and hastily stepped back. 'Forgive me, my lord, as you might imagine I am not feeling well after a long and tiring journey. Perhaps you would be kind enough to have me taken to a room?'

If he spoke, it would be to say something he would regret. He turned his back on her and strode to the sanctuary of the library, unable to comprehend what he'd just been told. How could he marry Eloise now, even if she would have him?

★　★　★

Eloise woke when the house was asleep. Apart from being a little light-headed, and having a raging thirst, she was perfectly well. It had been an error of judgement on her part to consume three glasses of champagne and she would not be so foolish again.

She was wide awake and scrambled out of bed. There was sufficient light from the fire to ignite a candle so she could see what time it was. Good heavens! She thought she had been asleep for hours and yet it was only eleven o'clock.

Her grandparents retired early but

she was certain Garrick would still be up. She wished to apologise and give him her word she would not be so immoderate again. She pushed her feet into her bed slippers and then found her robe. There was no necessity to take a candlestick as the sconces would be left burning.

With her stick in one hand, and the skirts of her robe and nightgown in the other, she headed for the staircase. The drawing room had been decorated after the family had gone to bed and it looked quite spectacular — even better than the grand hall. She paused long enough in the doorway to admire it and then made her way to the library, where she was certain he would be if he had not already gone to bed.

She pushed open the door and immediately saw he was stretched out on the leather sofa, a full glass of brandy in one hand and an empty decanter on the hexagonal table beside him. She had not thought him a drinker but he was certainly bosky.

'Garrick, I have come to speak to you. Are you capable of listening?'

He sat up so suddenly the glass flew from his hand and landed in the fire. The resulting explosion caused her to step back in shock. She missed her footing and tumbled to the floor. Her skirts fell into the flames and immediately caught fire.

Before she could react, he was beside her and she was unceremoniously rolled over and over in a large rug. 'Enough, I shall cast up my accounts if you continue. The flames are out and I am unharmed.'

He lifted her to her feet and then vanished behind the sofa where she heard a disgusting gurgling and retching sound. The smell was most unpleasant and she had no sympathy for his distress.

'I am going to the kitchen to make coffee. I suggest you join me when you're recovered.'

Her stick was propped against the sofa and she snatched it up and moved as quickly as she could to leave him to his unpleasant task. As soon as she was outside and the door closed firmly behind her she took several deep breaths.

There was a distinct smell of burnt material and she moved closer to the sconce in order to see the damage to her nightwear. Her head spun when she saw that half the front of her robe and her nightgown had gone, leaving just the charred remains behind.

If he had not moved so quickly she would have been hideously burnt, possibly fatally. Of course, she would not have been placed in such danger if he had not been so drunk he had tossed his brandy into the flames.

So shocked was she by her narrow escape that all desire for coffee vanished and she decided to return to her chamber. To her astonishment she saw a woman in her nightclothes walk boldly into his apartment as if she had every right to be there.

She opened her mouth to call out but then thought better of it. There was something havey-cavey going on and she was quite certain Garrick's drunkenness was linked to this mysterious woman. It took her less than ten minutes to find the necessary undergarments and a gown she could slip on over her head. Her hair would have to remain in a braid dangling down her back.

Whilst she was dressing, she believed she had unravelled the mystery. This was Garrick's mistress and she had come to ruin their wedding. This was not going to happen. If she could vanquish ghosts then a woman with no reputation should be a mere bagatelle.

11

Eloise followed this light-skirt into Garrick's bedroom. The wretched woman was draped across his bed with more of her flesh on show than was seemly. This would not do — it would not do at all. She looked around the room and saw a jug of water left on the washstand for his ablutions when he retired.

She picked it up and, before the intruder could react, hurled the contents over her. The woman screamed and leapt from the bed, her scarlet silk peignoir quite ruined.

'I know who you are and why you have come here. Nothing you can say or do will prevent Lord Forsyth and I getting married on Monday. How in God's name you come to be in this house I don't know — but I shall have you physically removed at first light.' Her voice was commendably firm and as she was leaning against the corner of the bed, her disability would not be obvious.

'I am Lady Sarah Dunstable and I am carrying the future Lord Forsyth.'

'If indeed you are with child, madam, you are carrying his bastard. If you don't wish to raise the infant yourself then I shall be happy to do so. He or she will be treated the same way as any of his or her future brothers or sisters.'

There was a sound behind her and her reprehensible husband-to-be arrived at her side. His arms came around her waist and she leaned back, revelling in his warmth and strength. He ignored his erstwhile lover.

'Are you quite sure you still wish to marry me?'

'I have never been so certain. It is unfortunate that this person has chosen to come here but she will be gone first thing in the morning.'

'How dare you talk about me as if I was of no account? I am the daughter of an earl. You cannot dismiss me so easily and I shall ruin Forsyth's name if he does not marry me and legitimise his child.'

His arms tightened and she knew he was having trouble controlling his temper. She squeezed his hands, letting him know that whatever was said or done it made no difference to her.

'Do you honestly think that anything you might say will cause my family harm? To my certain knowledge, I am your third lover since your husband died. Your reputation is non-existent and you are not received in any of the best drawing rooms. You have failed in your endeavour.'

Whilst he had been speaking, something else occurred to Eloise. 'How is it that you have been intimate with so many gentlemen and never produced a baby? Yet fortuitously, just as Lord Penston is about to marry, you find yourself in an interesting condition?'

'Come, darling girl, we need to talk.' He ignored Lady Sarah and drew her lovingly out of the room. As one they turned and left the wretched woman in his bedchamber to contemplate her folly.

'Garrick, did my grandparents witness her arrival?'

'No, they retired immediately after dinner. Unfortunately, the two servants who were in the hall heard everything.'

'They will not gossip. Everyone who has remained is loyal to the family. Do you really think you should leave her in your apartment? She might well destroy your entire wardrobe and anything else she might lay her hands on.'

Then his valet stepped out of the sitting room. 'If you will allow me to, my lord, I can deal with this problem for you and no one will be any the wiser in the morning?'

'You will have my eternal gratitude if you can do so without rousing the entire household. How do you intend to achieve this miracle?'

'The trunks are back on the carriage; the horses are about to be harnessed again. Her own maid has her garments ready in the bedchamber she was allocated. I have three other stout fellows waiting to assist.'

'Lady Sarah must not be harmed in any way. She is misguided but I forgive her breach of manners.' Eloise meant every word. The poor woman must really love Garrick to have attempted such a trick.

'Her ladyship will be treated with respect, miss, but she will leave here tonight.'

Satisfied that things were being taken care of, she left this competent manservant to his task.

When they were safely inside her sitting room she stepped away and viewed him with disfavour. 'I am most displeased with you, Lord Penston. It's not the fact that your former mistress came to ruin our wedding but the fact that you drank yourself into a stupor and then were horribly sick in my presence.'

Now she could see him clearly, it was apparent he looked decidedly unwell. He had hit his head twice in the past week. Could this be why he was so pale and desperate looking? Then he brushed his eyes and she saw his cheeks were wet.

'Garrick, my love, what is wrong?'

He shook his head, too overcome to speak. She threw her arms around him, unbearably moved by his tears. She was crushed against him and then lifted and in two strides they were on the daybed together.

'My darling, how can you be so sanguine about this disaster? To offer to raise another woman's child — I cannot understand why you would do so. Any other young lady would have sent me packing.'

'We love each other and that's all that matters to me. You accepted me without hesitation despite my infirmity. Did you honestly think I would not do the same for you?'

'I thought you lost to me and tried to drown my sorrows. Then when your robe caught fire my head cleared and I was able to put the flames out. I sincerely apologise for my disgusting behaviour afterwards. The shock of what might have happened overcame me.'

She settled more comfortably in his arms. 'I rather think it was the excess of brandy that overcame you, my love, but we will let that pass. I'm surprised you don't smell more unpleasant than you do.'

His chuckle told her he was recovering his spirits. 'Thank you for reminding me, sweetheart. I shall endeavour to improve the matter.'

He gently removed her from his lap and vanished into her bedroom. Whilst she listened to him washing she realised he had nowhere to sleep tonight. She limped to the doorway and her breath caught in her throat.

He was standing in just his unmentionables, his magnificent torso naked. He glanced over his shoulder and his expression changed. His eyes darkened and a hectic flush ran along his cheekbones.

Her feet moved of their own volition and she literally fell into his outstretched arms.

★   ★   ★

They were roused the following morning by the sound of a tray of chocolate
and morning rolls being dropped on the
boards. Polly threw her apron over her
head and ran from the room.

'Oh dear! I had quite forgotten my
maid came in so early.' Eloise made no
attempt to remove herself from his arms.
This was where she was meant to be.

'You have made me the happiest of
men — I did not think I could ever feel
this way.' His wicked smile made his
intentions clear.

'We should get up. You should return
to your apartment immediately. There
has been more than enough scandal in
this house already.'

'Too late to repine, my darling, I love
you and I'm going nowhere.'